13

93

ROBBERY AT GLENROCK

JIM BOWDEN

A Black Horse Western

ROBERT HALE · LONDON

© Jim Bowden 1992
First published in Great Britain 1992

ISBN 0 7090 4760 6

Robert Hale Limited
Clerkenwell House
Clerkenwell Green
London EC1R 0HT

Photoset in North Wales by
Derek Doyle & Associates, Mold, Clwyd.
Printed and bound in Great Britain by
WBC Ltd, Bridgend, Glamorgan.

ONE

The taller of the two guards, sweating heavily in the heat of the day, stepped past the prisoner and rapped on the brown door, its colour matching the sombre look and barred windows of the corridor.

The second guard, alert, his hand resting on the butt of his Colt, stood behind the prisoner.

Red Collins, his round face thinning after two years in this hell-hole of a gaol, his hands, hard from wielding a sledgehammer in the quarry, his clothes, torn and dusty, his feet swollen in boots designed to make it difficult for the prisoner to run, licked his lips, parched by the blazing sun.

The guard pushed open the door in answer to the shout of, 'Come in.' He entered the room, stood to one side of the door, turned and indicated to the prisoner to walk in. His eyes were cold, with no emotion, as he watched Collins shuffle past him.

Red knew the drill. He had been before the governor several times – the first few occasions, shortly after he had been condemned for bank robbery, resulted in stern disciplinary measures for trying to kick against the system. More recently the visits had been congratulatory on the way he had learned his lessons and had settled down.

Red had come to the conclusion that it only made things worse for himself to try to buck the authority of the prison. This was no weakening on the part of the man who had twelve bank robberies to his credit, rather it showed a strength of reasoning, for good conduct could bring him a remission, for there burned deep in his heart revenge on the men who had condemned him to this living hell – the lawman, the judge and the governor who now sat behind his big desk eyeing the prisoner as he shambled into the room.

Collins stopped half-way between the door and the desk, precisely on a black cross marked on the floor for this purpose, so placed that the prisoner would have no chance of attacking the governor before he would be gunned down by the guards.

The second guard moved into the room and closed the door.

There was a mixture of hate and curiosity in Collins's dark brown eyes as he stared impassively at the small, stocky man behind the desk.

The governor met that stare with a coldness which would have sent shivers down many a prisoner's spine. Curt Muller hated his job and had nothing but contempt for the men under his authority. He had entered the prison service as the only work he could get as an East European who had come to a 'promised land' which he found held no promise. It bred in him a hate of his fellow men and a determination to achieve something from the profession forced upon him by necessity. So he had set his eyes on becoming a governor, in which position he could wield god-like power without mercy over fellow human beings. Now those days were coming to an end. Retirement was being forced upon him by higher authority which had little concern for his future welfare.

Muller revelled in the silence. Let the prisoner stew for a few moments; let him wonder why he had been sent for; let him anticipate solitary confinement. Muller delighted in this silent torture and now he savoured it all the more for he knew there would not be many more of these moments.

His grey eyes were fixed firmly on Collins. Though he knew Red had a determined mind there never had been a prisoner who had out-stared him. There was something about those cold, grey eyes – the lack of sympathy, the absence of any sort of feeling – which made a man divert his look. It was as if those eyes were tearing the very soul out of the prisoner.

Red stared back as he always did. He held firm. The tension mounted with eyes locked on each other. Then Red felt an uneasiness stirring from his very depths. His facial muscles twitched. Muller knew the signs. His eyes pierced even more intently. Red could stand it no longer. His eyes flickered and turned away. Then they were back, fixed on the governor, but the spell had been broken.

Red's mouth tightened. He swayed forward as if he would leap when he saw the amused triumph flick the governor's lips whose eyes still showed no emotion.

'Don't try it, Collins!' The words came in a sharp whisper from one of the guards and Red knew there would be a Colt trained on the middle of his back.

Muller grinned, easing the tension but then he brought it back with a sharp snap which chilled the prisoner's heart. The governor's smile vanished leaving the icy greyness penetrating Red's very soul. His lips curled in contempt as he relished the power he was about to brandish.

'Collins, I'm moving you to Rock Springs today.' Muller let the words wrap coldly around the prisoner at the same time incising them on his very heart.

For a split moment Collins did not seem to take the meaning in. Then the words made their impact. His heart missed a beat; he gasped, his intake of breath revealing the shock. His stomach knotted. Nausea rose in him but exploded into anger.

'You can't! Why? What the hell have I done?' His eyes smouldered with a hate which would have been assuaged only in a violent vengeance had the cold muzzle of a Colt not been pressing into his back. His body trembled with helpless frustration. The man seated before him was acting as accuser, jury and judge and relishing every second of the prisoner's reaction.

'I can and I am,' replied Muller, enjoying the power in those simple words.

'Not Rock Springs! Not that Hades!'

'Yes!'

'But why? What have I done? My disruptive days are over. You talked to me before and I realized I couldn't outsmart you and the system you ran here. You broke me, damn you, you broke me and now this!' Red's words came fast, hurled at the governor in desperation.

Muller leaned forward, his elbows resting on the desk, his finger tips pressed together. He looked over them with narrowed eyes.

'I don't believe you Collins, never have. I didn't break you. You decided to behave when you realized you were no longer a big shot and couldn't outsmart me. You still seethe underneath. You're still a potential trouble-maker but I aim to see that you don't get the chance; that you are broken once and for all and are no longer a menace to society.' Muller leaned back in his chair, his hands coming slowly to rest on its arms. It was a deliberate movement of satisfaction as he drew pleasure from the fear which stalked in Collins's face.

That fear came with the knowledge of what a move to Rock Springs meant. Red had heard of its reputation as a prison run by the most sadistic guards west of the North Platte. Punishments were meted out for the slightest reason and the guards were inventive. Few men left Rock Springs alive and if they did they were completely broken, physically and mentally.

'You've got it all wrong. I'm not a trouble-maker. I know when I'm beat and I knew that weeks ago. I …'

'You've only just decided to realize it,' hissed Muller with contempt.

'No. No. You're wrong.' Red saw his protest was falling on stony ground and decided to change his attitude. 'Please, Mr Muller, not to Rock Springs. I'll give you my word, I'll …'

'Word!' Muller's lips curled into a disbelieving sneer. 'Your word? It's not worth the air it's breathed on.'

'It is! It is! I promise. I promise. I'll be a model prisoner.' Collins clenched his fists pleadingly; his face contorted in anguish and his eyes held the baleful look of a man clinging to one last shred of hope.

Muller watched Collins with scorn, enjoying the sight of a man, once regarded as one of the toughest bank robbers in the country, grovelling and pleading with *him*, Curt Muller, who had been derided and shunned by this man's fellow countrymen.

Muller let his no comment worm in the prisoner's

10

mind.

'Don't condemn me to hell. Don't send me to Rock Springs. Please, I beg you, don't do it. You've no reason.'

'I don't need a reason. What I decide will be!'

The incisive words sent a chill through Red. All energy drained from him. His body felt as if it had been pounded into nothing. He sank on to his knees, his body bent. He shuddered with sobs of despair.

Curt Muller pushed himself to his feet and moved slowly round the desk until he stood in front of a man beaten by the knowledge of his fate.

The two guards, alert to the nearness of the governor to the prisoner, moved on either side of the man on the floor.

Muller stared down at Collins and enjoyed the sight of a man grovelling at his feet. 'You will leave at noon.' He savoured each word, his final gesture of power. He glanced up at the guards. 'Get him out of here.'

'On your feet!' The first guard prodded Red with his Colt. Red did not move.

'Up!' The second guard stabbed Red with his boot. Red remain in the same position, his body shaking.

'I said get him out of here!' Muller snapped impatiently.

The two guards glanced at each other. They knew that when the governor spoke you jumped to it without any delay. They both bent down and each grabbed Red by a shoulder and dragged him to his feet and at the same time started for the door.

The action awoke the fighting streak in Collins. With his face creased in a snarl like some cornered wild animal, he struggled to break free, but his weakened state could not shake the guards' firm grip. Their step hardly faltered.

'You can't do this,' yelled Red, his eyes burning with utter hatred at the governor. 'One day I'll get you Muller! One day you'll beg for mercy! And you won't get it!'

The guard jerked the door open and the two men hauled Red into the corridor. His last sight of the governor was of two grey eyes piercing his very soul.

The prison clock struck twelve. Curt Muller rose from his chair and crossed the floor to the window which looked down into the prison yard. Directly opposite, the huge, studded doors in the prison gate were being swung back as the prison wagon rumbled towards them. A driver and two guards, rifles across their knees, sat on the seat which formed part of the main iron construction, built to transport six prisoners at a time. Now it contained only one.

Drawn by four horses, it trundled through the gate.

'Enjoy the iron whore,' called one of the gate guards. He gave a mocking laugh at the thought of the uncomfortable ride on top of the wagon.

'Swop you places,' suggested one of the guards as he shuffled to find a more comfortable position.

'Not bloody likely,' came the reply.

Inside, Red Collins lay on the metal floor. He didn't even want to look out of the tiny barred opening in the door. His thoughts were a turmoil, alternating between utter desolation and a determination to survive, no matter what, so that he could seek revenge on the men who had condemned him to hell.

The wagon creaked beyond the gateway.

The gates swung shut.

The wagon was gone from the governor's sight. When he turned from the window there was a smile on his face. The grey eyes were no longer cold for they anticipated a retirement of leisure on the ten thousand dollars which he knew would be in a bank account in Rawlins tomorrow.

TWO

The prison wagon had been travelling two hours. The pace was slow for the wagon was heavy. The forward movement created no respite in the hot still air. The three men seated high on the wagon cursed the governor for ordering the prisoner to be transferred during the hottest part of the day.

Muller had no consideration for them. His only thought had been for his own sadistic pleasure in knowing how a fellow human being would be suffering. The guards were hot but even their hard hearts went out to Red for he would be cooking. True he was not exposed to the direct rays of the sun as they were but the inside of the wagon would be like an oven, and there would be little air from the one tiny, barred opening in the door.

One of the guards tipped his water bottle to his lips for the tenth time. The other eased his stetson and mopped his brow. The driver drooped; horses at this pace took no handling. The three men anticipated no trouble. No one knew the prisoner was being moved. The driver could have managed on his own; there was no chance of Red breaking out, but the governor had ordered two guards to accompany the wagon and no one argued with the governor.

The wagon trundled along the rutted trail, each hole, each hump buffeting the prisoner who had soon given up trying to find a position which would ease his discomfort. He lay, unresisting to the wagon's movements, staring unseeingly at the roof. Sweat poured from him. It ran from his brow into his eyes. His clothes, such as they were, stuck to his sweat-soaked body. He gasped for air. Soon after they had left the prison he had hauled himself to the small opening and gulped at the air but there was little to ease his torture and he had long given up trying. He closed his eyes trying to shut out the torments of the journey but they were ever-present, mocking him, trying to drive his mind beyond the edge of sanity. He fought them with thoughts of the pleasure he was going to derive from the revenge he would wreak, but then they would win and, as now, he would sink into a deep depression of despair with no hope. A life of torment, of pain, of utter dejection, a life where all self-respect and dignity were submerged in a morass of evil abuse.

His thoughts tore at his mind driving him to look around for something to end it all, but there was nothing. The inside of the wagon was constructed without any projection which could offer a prisoner an easy way out.

Red yelled at the top of his voice, heaping curses on the men who had driven him to this but no one heard, the words merely came back to him from the sides of his tomb-like box.

The words faded on his lips. The wagon had stopped, bringing with it relief from the bruising jolting. Voices. The noise penetrated his mind, driving away his horrific thoughts.

'Get down. Easy like.'

Then a voice nearer. 'Red Collins?'

Red raised his head to see the muzzle of a Colt poking between the bars of the opening in the door and behind it part of a face.

What the hell was going on? Red hesitated. Admit he was Red Collins and he might be blasted by that Colt. But why? Say he wasn't and he might just as easily be gunned down. How could he know what the face behind the gun intended?

'Who wants to know?' he gasped.

'Ain't none of your business. Just answer the question.'

Red's swollen tongue tried to moisten his lips. He saw no reason to deny his identity. 'Yes,' he croaked.

To his relief the gun was withdrawn and the voice said, 'We'll have you out in a minute.'

The words drove life coursing through his veins. Out! Out of this coffin! Free! No Rock Springs!

Red couldn't believe it. His mind tried to grasp what was happening. Maybe he was delirious, lost in the imaginings of a tortured mind. He struggled to his feet and stumbled to the tiny opening. He wasn't a raving lunatic. There was somebody outside.

'Move!' The word came harsh, commanding.

There was movement to the back of the wagon but Red couldn't see what was going on.

'Keys.'

A moment later a man, the lower half of his face covered by his bandanna, came into view. A key rattled in a lock, then a second one did the same. The door swung open.

Red stared. This wasn't really happening. A few moments ago he was entombed, crushed, defeated. Now space had suddenley opened up before him. He could step into it. Freedom beckoned.

Red hesitated, holding on to the side of the wagon, shielding his eyes against the harsh light of the afternoon sun. He breathed deeply. Though the air was hot it was fresh compared to that he had endured in the iron box. He felt energy being driven into his body.

'Take it easy. Let me help you down.' The voice of the masked man was friendly.

Hands reached out to help him to the ground. He stretched and was aware of two other men, bandannas over their faces, controlling five horses while another, with Colt held ready, stood close to the driver and the two guards.

18

The man, who had unlocked the wagon and helped him down, drew his Colt. 'Inside,' he rapped.

The three men who had been escorting the prisoner shuffled forward and climbed into the wagon. The door clanged shut and the keys were turned in the locks.

The rescuers holstered their guns. 'You all right?' one of them, whom Red took to be the leader, asked.

'Sure am, now I'm out of that hole,' replied Red, feeling stronger with every passing second and the realization that this was really happening to him. 'What's this all about?'

'You'll find out before long,' came the reply. The man turned and nodded to the man who had helped Red to the ground. He went to the front of the wagon and climbed on to the driving-seat. Gathering up the reins he sent the horses forward and after a few yards turned them off the trail to a dip in the land where the vehicle was hidden from the trail. He halted the horses and hurried back to join the others.

As the wagon moved away Red took in his immediate surroundings. They were beside a wide tree-lined stream at a point where the trail forded the water. This was rolling grassland with distant mountains filling the western horizon. He sensed his rescuers relax once the wagon had disappeared from sight. He was curious to know who they were but when they removed their bandannas he was no wiser for he did not know any of them.

He turned to the man he took to be the leader. 'I'm sure glad to be free but what's going on? I don't know you. I'm curious, why bust me?'

The man grinned. 'All in good time. We've some fresh clothes for you. There's some water there,' he inclined his head towards the stream, 'and I figure you might enjoy it.'

'I sure would.' Red could not believe his luck. He still expected to wake up from some delirium and find himself being shaken by that rumbling oven of a wagon. He peeled off his shirt and trousers and ran to the deeper water he had spotted downstream of the ford. With a great whoop he jumped in and when he surfaced he flung water over and over his head. The water tanged his body with its cooling chill, bliss after the oppressive heat of the iron box. The last time he had experienced the delight of cooling water was over two years ago and now he made the most of it.

The leader of his rescuers sat on the bank side. 'I reckon we ought to introduce ourselves. I'm Clem Adams.'

Red nodded. He now had time to observe the men who had rescued him from the pestilent pit to which that bastard of a governor had condemned him. Clem was tall, slim, but in that slimness was a steel-like strength and in his eyes was an alertness which would miss nothing. He impressed Red as a man who could make a quick decision and be right.

'Fella in the check shirt,' Clem indicated one of the two men with the horses, 'Walt Bingham.'

Bingham raised his hand in acknowledgement. He was stocky, with the toughness of rawhide about him. Red noted that apart from a Colt, positioned low to adjust to his long arms, Walt also had a knife sheathed to his belt.

'The other's Cadiz,' said Clem.

Red nodded to him and received in return a broad grin which revealed perfect teeth. He was the youngest, and also the best looking. Red guessed no more than twenty-two, and figured that his good looks came from a Mexican mother. His swarthy features were handsomely chiselled and his eyes flashed with a carefree enjoyment of life. Careless? Red reckoned not for he could sense a coiled spring behind the relaxed appearance.

'And, this here's Dex Duran.' Clem indicated the man who had driven the wagon away. 'All fixed, Dex?'

'Sure, out of sight of the trail. Won't be found until they realize at Rock Springs that they aren't going to have the pleasure of Red's company.' The words came with a lazy drawl and a grin.

'I sure won't miss them,' laughed Red. He watched Dex squat beside Clem. He figured there was a strong relationship between these two, maybe they had ridden the trail together for some time. Dex matched Clem for height but he was broader.

His face was lean, hard-boned; his eyes, deep set, had an almost dreamy look but Red saw they were sharp, their glances incisive, making a summary and judgement in an instance.

'Want a shave?' Clem asked as he indicated the brush, soap, cut-throat razor and mirror lying on the bank side.

'Sure would,' replied Red. He wallowed in the river, close to the bank as he rid himself of the unsightly growth. He swilled his face and started to move from the water. Even as he climbed up the bank he felt the sun drying him. After a brisk rub-down he dressed quickly in the new clothes provided for him.

'Not a bad fit,' he commented as he tightened the belt around his waist. 'How d'you know my size?'

'We made it our business to know,' replied Clem.

Red eyed him. 'All thoroughly planned. What's behind all this? Why spring me? And how d'you know I'd be in that hell-oven of a wagon?'

Clem leaned back on his elbows and met Red's searching eyes. 'I've told you, all in good time. Now we ride.' He started to swing to his feet.

'Hold it,' snapped Red. 'I'd like to know what I'm getting into. What do you want me for?'

Clem straightened. His eyes hardened. 'Look, Collins, ain't you glad to be free? We can just as easily put you back in that wagon.'

'You won't,' Red replied, a mocking grin twitching the corners of his lips. 'You want me for

22

something special or you wouldn't have busted me out, so you ain't going to put me back, just like that.'

'Maybe,' said Clem coldly. 'But don't get big ideas about yourself. There'll come a time when you'll have served your purpose.'

Red stiffened at the threat behind the words. 'What if I don't like what you want?'

Clem grinned. 'Oh, you'll like or you're right back in the calaboose.'

'Try me.'

'Ain't my job.'

'So you ain't running this show.' Red seized on the information, feeling in a much stronger situation with the knowledge that Clem wasn't the boss.

'I do for the boss, and let me make it clear right now, you don't buck my orders.' His words were emphasized, sharp and clear. They left Red in no doubt that to cross Clem would be crossing the man at the top, the man who had planned his escape.

'All right, Clem. I'm sorry, but you know how it is, one minute stewing in that iron box, the next free; it's a bit heady and I just wondered ...'

'Save it,' cut in Clem. 'No harm done, reckon we understand each other a bit better. Now, let's ride.'

Red nodded, picked up the stetson and crammed it on his head. 'No Colt?' His words were half question, half comment.

'You'll get one at the right time,' replied Clem as he swung into the saddle.

'When the boss says so,' answered Red, unable to

keep the touch of sarcasm out of his voice.

Clem stiffened, then leaned forward on his saddle horn. 'That's right,' he said coldly. 'And if I recommend him not to let you have one you won't get one. Now, quit bucking the fact that you're free.' Clem pulled his horse round and sent it across the ford.

The other three sent their mounts splashing through the water.

Red shrugged his shoulders. He had nothing to lose by riding with them, maybe a lot to gain. He had tested the leader, knew he was a man to be reckoned with and from the actions of the other three during the exchange of words, he realized they would back Clem. Besides, he was curious about several aspects of the recent happenings. Who wanted him badly enough to plan his escape? And why? And how did they know he was being moved from the pen?

Red stabbed his horse forward, the clop of the hooves on the stony river bed marking a change in his fortunes. Red grinned. He'd sure make the most of what lay before him and then – that revenge which still burned deep within him.

THREE

They rode at a steady pace for an hour before Clem called a halt, in a hollow beside a stream.

There had been little conversation throughout the ride and, though Red tried to elicit more information as to who was behind his freedom and why, none of his rescuers would be drawn. Finally he gave up, knowing that his curiosity would be salved when the time was ready.

'Twenty minutes,' called Clem as he swung from the saddle and allowed his horse freedom to drink from the stream.

The others did likewise and slaked their thirst from the clear running water. Clem scooped some water into his stetson and poured it over his head. As he ran his hand through his hair the heat of the sun was already drying it. He opened one of his saddlebags and took out some jerky.

'Red,' he called and, as Red straightened from the water, he tossed a piece to him. 'Chew on that.'

Red caught the piece of dried meat. 'Thanks.

How much further?'

'Couple of hours.'

Red grimaced with surprise. 'Reckon I'll need this.' He nodded his thanks and took a bite of the jerky.

The men, thankful to be out of the saddle for a while, stretched themselves in the shade of some cottonwoods which lined the stream.

Red, gazing upwards at the blue beyond the branches, relaxed and revelled in his freedom. A short while ago he was roasting in an iron box, now he was free, free from the confining space of prison, free! But how free? Red's thoughts suddenly jerked his racing mind to a stop. He was beholden to someone, someone who wanted him out of prison. What for? What price would he have to pay?

'All right, let's ride.' Clem's call interrupted Red's thoughts.

He was no nearer solving the questions which dogged him but now, back in the saddle, he knew he was moving towards the answers.

Nearly two hours later, Clem called a halt at the top of a rise.

Red took in the scene swiftly. The hill dropped gently to a river valley. Beyond it the land rose in a series of heightening hills to a distant horizon of blue-hazed mountains. On the far side of the river, sheltering in a curve in the hill stood a long, low, ranch house. To its left, about two hundred yards away, lay another long building which, on seeing two men emerge, Red reckoned was the bunkhouse. Further to the left Red saw the stables with three corrals close by.

A track led from the ranch to follow the flow of the river to the right. Red saw that it passed through a gateway in a fence to join a trail which swung down from the hill, follow the river and disappear round the curve of the hill on which they were standing.

'Nice spot,' commented Red.

'End of our ride,' said Clem.

Red's glance at Clem was a mixture of curiosity and suspicion. 'Hey, I'm no cowpuncher.'

A smile flicked Cadiz's lips, 'We wouldn't have busted him out of gaol if he had been, would we Clem?'

'Sure wouldn't,' grinned Clem.

'Then why?' Red looked round his rescuers. If they had risked their necks for his talents, then that meant bank robbing – but that ranch down there seemed no place for a bank robber.

'You'll soon find out.' Clem sent his horse down the slope. The others followed.

Clem swung to the river opposite the house and put his mount at the water. They splashed their way across the convenient ford and rode up to the house.

As they approached it a broad, thickset man came on to the veranda and strode with a deliberate step to the rail. He leaned on it, studying one rider in particular.

Red reckoned this was the man he had been brought to see, that this was the man who had masterminded his escape. He knew he was under scutiny and he returned that study.

The man exuded the power of authority even from this distance. Red figured he would brook no nonsense, that what he said was law and he knew that, whatever the reason for breaking him out of that hell-hole of a gaol, this man would expect repayment in full and more. As they neared the veranda, Red saw the man's eyes were sharp, that there was muscular power in the body and he reckoned this man could take care of himself if the necessity arose, but that was unlikely for his authority would command men, like these riders, to deal with any trouble.

Clem pulled to a halt in front of the veranda.

The man straightened. His rugged features were square-jawed, his eyebrows bushy, matching his light brown hair. 'Any trouble, Clem?'

'None, Mr Palmer. The set-up was perfect.'

'Good.' The man nodded and swept his gaze across the other three riders. 'Thanks,' he said. While the word was one of appreciation it was also one of dismissal. Walt, Cadiz and Dex turned their horses and rode towards the stables. The man turned his attention to Red. 'Climb down and come inside, Collins. You too Clem.' He turned and, without waiting for them, went into the house.

Red glanced at Clem who nodded and swung from his saddle. Red tied his horse to the hitching-rail and followed Clem up the steps on to the veranda. When they entered the house, Clem led the way across the square hall on the floor of which three brightly coloured rugs were casually scattered. A small table stood against one wall with a high backed chair at each end.

The room, in which they found Palmer waiting, was comfortably furnished with four large chairs ranged in an arc around the fireplace and its heavily carved wooden surround. Across one corner stood a large mahogany desk. A table occupied one wall and framed paintings of western scenes decorated the walls.

Red felt a little nervous. It was a long time since he had been in a house of this elegance. He wondered what the owner of such a spread could want with the likes of him.

'Red Collins, welcome to the Running W.' The man held out his hand and Red felt a strong, firm grip. 'Matt Palmer.'

'Glad to know you Mr Palmer,' said Red. 'Guess you must be behind these fellas bustin' me out of gaol.'

'You guess right,' returned Matt.

'Then, thanks. I'm mighty grateful. But why? What the hell d'you want with me? I'm not cut out for punching cattle.'

29

Matt chuckled. 'With your record, I reckon not.' He moved behind his desk and sat down on the armchair. He indicated the two high-backed chairs in front of the desk. Red and Clem sat down.

'I want you for a special purpose, Red. Sure, this is a cattle ranch. Clem here and his three sidekicks have little to do with it unless there's trouble. They are my trouble-shooters. I have other interests, some of them in Creston, our nearest town, five miles from here.'

'So, where do I fit in?' said Red. 'I reckon you didn't get me here just to ride with Clem.'

'Right again,' said Matt, reaching forward to select a cheroot from a box on the desk. He leaned back in his chair.

'And how did you know I was being moved to Rock Springs? You must have done to arrange what you did.'

'I have contacts.'

Red's mind was racing with ideas. He had been moved the same day as the governor had made his decision. Muller must have made his mind up beforehand. He would be the only one who would know about the move. So was Muller the contact?

'The governor?' Red asked, his eyes widening with curiosity.

Matt nodded. 'Let's say I make it my business to know a man's weaknesses if I want anything. It was you I wanted so I did a little persuading along with some suggestions. And here you are.'

'Well I'll be damned! I guess I'll have to take Muller off my hit list.'

'Hit list? You want revenge?'

'The sheriff who hauled me in, the judge who put me in that pig of a gaol and the governor who gave me hell. Well I reckon I'll have to forget Muller.'

'I reckon you will,' said Matt. He struck a match and lit his cheroot, all the time eyeing Red, making his own judgement on the man he had only heard about. His eyes narrowed. 'If you work for me, you forget that hit list.'

'I want those bastards!' snapped Red, stiffening at Palmer's ban.

'Understandable,' said Matt. 'But save it until after my job's through.

'What do I get out of this?' Red was beginning to feel more at ease, boosted by the fact that he must have something which this man wanted desperately enough to risk bribing a prison governor.

'You'll be well paid,' replied Matt testily, sensing the touch of arrogance coming into Red's attitude.

'How much?' insisted Red, running his hand through his hair.

'That depends on a number of things, one of which is how much you have to give. Clem will vouch I'm fair.'

'That's right, Red. You'll come out of it all right,' confirmed Clem, glancing at Red.

'So what do you want?' asked Red.

'I want your assurance that you'll ride for me.' Matt's eyes narrowed as he watched Collins intently.

'Why should I commit myself before knowing what you want?' asked Red, cautious about what he might be getting into.

Matt leaned forward on the desk. 'Because you ain't getting to know my plans unless you're committed to me.' His voice penetrated, demanding an instant decision from Red.

'And supposing I turn you down?' Red fenced.

'Does that gaol tempt you back?' The cold tone bit deep into Red's mind.

'Hell! You wouldn't!' gasped Red his eyes widening with disbelief and horror.

'Be easier than busting you out,' hissed Matt, his lips curling with contempt at the fact that Red had presumed he was completely free. 'My men caught you on the run. You could tell your tale but who'd believe YOU?'

Red licked his lips. He was cornered. He knew it was no use kicking against Palmer, who held all the aces. He would have to curb his natural suspicion of all men in this case. Maybe Palmer would deal him a straight hand if he rode with him.

'All right,' Red agreed reluctantly.

'You work for me. No questions asked. You take orders from me or from Clem. Step out of line and you're finished.' Matt's voice was firm. He would brook no nonsense and Red knew it from his tone and the cold piercing look in his eyes.

Red nodded.

'Right.' Matt eased into a more amiable attitude. 'Well, the first thing which concerns you is that I want some information.'

Red looked at Matt with curiosity. What information could he have which was of use to this rancher?

'Where's your brother?'

Red was startled by the question and went immediately on the defensive. Wes had been the one to escape after the bank robbery, and Wes had had the $100,000! Is that what Palmer was after?

'What do you want him for?' Suspicion showed in Red's voice.

'Later,' rapped Matt, brushing aside Red's question. 'Do you know where he is?'

'No.'

'You know where he might be?' pressed Matt.

Red ignored Matt's probing and countered with his own question. 'Have you tried to find him?'

Matt nodded. 'Yes, but after that robbery he vanished. I've not found a trace of him. It's as if he'd left this earth.'

'So when you drew a blank, you thought of me.' Anger welled in Red. 'If you'd found him I'd still be rotting in gaol, you wouldn't have given me a thought. Damn you, Palmer. You find Wes.' Red stood up and would have stormed from the room but in that instance he saw Clem's Colt leave its leather and point at him.

'You're on the wrong end, Red, so sit down.' The words, soft but menacing, were heightened by the hard, threatening look in Clem's eyes.

Red sat down slowly.

'Don't get all het up, Collins,' snapped Matt. 'You ...'

'Het up!' broke in Red, his eyes blazing with fury. 'What do you damn well expect after what you implied?'

'I ain't implied anything – it's your interpretation,' rapped Matt.

'You expect me to tell you where you can find Wes so that you can get your hands on the cash we took from that bank!' Red snorted with contempt.

'There you go, jumping to conclusions again,' said Matt, shrugging his shoulders as if he had a hopeless case on his hands. 'I ain't interested in that cash. I want your brother because he has a reputation as the best with dynamite west of Laramie.'

Surprised, Red stared at Matt. 'What you got in mind?'

'I have a job that wants doing which needs an expert with dynamite – and I want the best. Your brother. So you tell me where I can find him.'

'Well, he could be in any of a dozen places.'

'Right, you go, get your bunk, some grub and figure out where we start to look for him and come back here and let me know.' Matt glanced at Clem and nodded.

Clem stood up and Red followed suit.

Matt eyed Red as the bank robber left the room. He'd have to keep his eye on this one. There was treachery deep in him and Matt reckoned Red would take easily to doublecrossing him.

'Don't buck Palmer, Red,' commented Clem as they led their horses to the stable. 'He can be mighty ruthless if anyone gets in his way or tries to pull something on him.'

Red made no comment. He didn't need Clem to tell him that. He had weighed Palmer up – a better friend than an enemy, but Red figured that once anyone had served their purpose Palmer would soon ditch them, one way or another.

After they had unsaddled their horses they left them in the care of the wrangler and made their way to the bunkhouse. Clem allocated a bunk to Red and took him to a room at the opposite end of the bunkhouse where they found Walt, Cadiz and Dex just finishing their meal of stew.

'Does he fit?' Walt directed his question at Clem with a nod in Red's direction.

'Sure I fit,' snapped Red before Clem could speak. 'I've got information Palmer wants, so I fit.'

'Don't get het up,' rapped Walt his eyes darkening as they met Red's. 'I only wanted to know, 'cos if you didn't fit I reckon we'd be taking you back to where we got you.'

Red stiffened. 'Don't reckon on that, you'd be dead first.'

Without taking his eyes off Red, Walt flicked his knife from his belt.

Red stepped back quickly, his body tense, every fibre keyed to meet Walt's attack. 'Take on an unarmed man?' he hissed.

Walt laughed, glanced down at his nails and started to clean one of them with the tip of the knife. Suddenly he raised his eyes at Red and in a movement, so swift that the eye could hardly take it in, he sent the knife flying past Red's right ear. Red started. His hand flew to his ear. He could have sworn the knife had nicked him but there was no blood when he looked at his hand.

'If you'd had a gun I'd have still beaten you,' grinned Walt. 'But you wouldn't have been feeling that ear.'

'You bastard.' Red swung round and lunged for the knife which had buried itself in the wall.

'Hold it!' Clem rapped. Red froze at the menace and demand. 'Ease off you two. Quit the play, Walt. If Red's riding with us we've all got to get along.'

'Right, boss.' Walt pushed himself to his feet to retrieve his knife. As he strolled past Red he grinned and winked at Red's tight-lipped glare.

Clem slipped his Colt back into its leather. 'Come on, Red, get some stew.'

They ladled some on to a plate and cut themselves a hunk of bread.

As they ate, Clem eased the tension with his talk.

As much as he hated having to bring in new riders, disturbing the understanding he had with his side-kicks of five years, he knew this was one time when he would have to keep things smooth. Palmer wanted this man so they'd have to get used to him. And he'd have to watch him. He'd heard of Red's reputation as a bank robber and knew he'd play on it. He was a rough, tough hombre who'd act first and think afterwards. He was known to be useful with a gun and would have no hesitation in using it. Clem figured there was a streak of treachery in Red, that he'd turn things to his own ends if necessary and his only loyalty would be to his own brother, and even that he doubted.

Red said little until he suddenly interrupted the flow of conversation between the other four. 'Palmer ain't all rancher, what else does he do?'

Clem swallowed a piece of meat. 'This here's a profitable working ranch, don't get any idea that it isn't.'

'Then why does he want you four?' cut in Red impatiently.

'Matt Palmer came to this land many years ago. He toiled hard to make his ranch successful. Don't know a lot about those early days but what I do know is that five years ago he was having trouble with neighbouring ranchers who were gradually trying to ease him out. We rode for him then, cleared up the trouble and he kept us on.'

'There must have been another reason for him to

do that.'

'Figured we'd be useful to see that his other interests ran smoothly.'

'Those are?'

'He's gradually bought up most of Creston and some people didn't and don't like it.'

'Didn't? That sounds as though you boys have been at work.'

'Like Clem said,' drawled Dex, 'Mr Palmer employed us to look after his interests.'

'And there's still trouble?'

'Could boil up at any time.'

'Where's my brother fit in?'

'Ain't fer us to say,' replied Clem. 'Matt has his own plans.'

'I'm sure you know more.'

Clem did not answer.

Red glanced round the four men. They didn't look hardcases but there certainly was an underlying toughness about them. Red reckoned if he didn't go along with Palmer they'd sure see that he was back in that gaol in quick time, and they'd no doubt claim the reward that was certain to be put out for him.

'Well, made up your mind?' asked Clem.

Red nodded and concentrated on the rest of his stew.

When he had finished, Clem eyed him. 'Want to see Mr Palmer now?'

'Yeah.'

A few minutes later the two men were back with the ranch owner.

'Reached a decision, Collins?' asked Matt.

'Yeah. I'll ride for you. Don't seem I've got much choice really, the cards are stacked against me.'

'Sure are,' grinned Matt, pushing himself to his feet and coming from behind his desk. He held out his hand. 'That seals it,' he said as Red took his hand. 'Play right by me and I'll see you well.' The warmth in Matt's deep blue eyes suddenly vanished leaving an icy coldness which emphasized the warning chill in Matt's voice. 'Cross me, and you'll regret it.' He turned away and returned to his seat motioning to the two men to sit down.

'Right, Collins. Where do I find your brother?'

'Wes could be anywhere.'

'I expect you to do better than that. You must have had some plans for your getaway after the robbery.'

'Sure but that was two years ago.'

'You had no communication from him while you were in prison?'

'None. We had this agreement if one of us was caught, no contact, just in case …'

'All right,' cut in Matt impatiently. 'Where were you going to hide out until the hunt cooled down?'

'We were to head down the North Platte for Riverside, there we head towards Bridger Peak, know of an old cabin north of the mountain.'

'Right, start there.'

'Wes wouldn't hole up there for two years.'

'Quit stalling, Red. Get to something more possible,' rapped Palmer, his eyes flaring with annoyance.

'All right, all right,' said Red, 'but let's work this thing through.'

'You know your brother's mind, you know his haunts, where would he likely go after Bridger Peak?'

'That's just what I'm trying to do,' said Red, an edge to his voice. 'Put myself in Wes's place.' He screwed his face thoughtfully. 'Reckon I'd have sat tight for a month.'

'Then?' prompted Matt.

'Well, I figure he'd ease his way south-east towards Pine Bluffs.'

'Why there?'

'Gal, Kate Conroe, he was kinda sweet on in Laramie, ran out on him when he made his first bank robbery. Only did it to get cash to make a home for her but she'd have none of it. He always said he'd find her again one day. We heard she was in Pine Bluffs so he figured one more bank and he'd quit, find her and persuade her he was going straight. I reckon if he's there he'd maybe take her name; wouldn't want Collins splashing around.'

'Right,' said Palmer, satisfaction in his voice. 'Start there. Clem you ride with him.'

'Sure, Mr Palmer. The others?'

'Leave 'em here, just in case there's any trouble.'

'Just one thing,' put in Red. 'I can't be sure Wes will come back with me. If he's found Kate, he might well have settled down. Understand, he's different from me. Me? I couldn't settle down like that. But Wes? Yes, he could.'

Matt leaned forward on his desk. 'You'll just have to persuade him. No matter what it takes or what you have to do, get him here or you end up back in that gaol.'

FOUR

After five days steady riding, wasting no time because of Matt Palmer's time limit of fourteen days, Red and Clem were pleased to have Pine Bluffs in sight. Red hoped his brother had found Kate and stayed put.

The town was small, boasting little more than a main street, a saloon, livery stable, hotel, and clapboard houses that looked in need of repair. The store signalled its purpose through peeling paint. A thin, gaunt faced man lounged on a chair beside the door and eyed the newcomers lazily from half-shut eyes.

'This gal chose a one-eyed place,' muttered Clem so that only Red could hear him as they halted in front of the store.

'Howdy,' called Red.

The storekeeper merely nodded in reply.

'Know a gal name of Kate Conroe?' asked Red.

'Might,' returned the man laconically. 'Conroe?

43

Rings a bell somewhere. Ask the wife, she's in the store.'

Red tossed his reins to Clem and swung from the saddle. He strode up the two steps on to the sidewalk and entered the store without a glance at the man in the chair.

'G'day, ma'am,' he called to the woman behind the counter who was straightening some bolts of cloth. She looked as though she could do with a new dress from some of it. She brushed the straggling, greying wisps of hair from her forehead as Red approached. 'Your husband said you might be able to help. We looking for a gal name of Kate Conroe.'

The woman looked thoughtful for a moment and then her face brightened with remembrance. 'Kate, a course I remember Kate, nice lass, but she left here a few years ago, just after her brother arrived.'

'Brother?' Red was puzzled, then he played a hunch. 'Oh, her brother Wes.'

'Sure, that was his name.'

'Know where they went?' he pressed.

'Not certain, but Kate had been saying that she was thinking of moving to Greeley. Can't blame her. This town was stagnating, Greeley was growing. Wanted my old man to move there but he wouldn't, lazy sod. Does nothing but sit on that damned chair all day.' Her mouth curled at the corners with contempt.

Red couldn't care less about her opinion of her husband, he had the information he wanted. 'Thanks ma'am,' he said and, swinging on his heels, he hurried from the store.

'Got it,' he called to Clem as he swung into the saddle. 'Greeley.'

The two men turned their horses without a glance at the storekeeper who tipped his battered, stained hat across his eyes, a symbol of Pine Bluffs which, like him, seemed to have lost its way.

'She left with her brother just after he arrived a few years back,' Red informed Clem.

'Brother?' But he's no damned use,' frowned Clem.

'Kate ain't any brothers,' replied Red. 'And the fella she left with is called Wes! We've got him, Clem.'

The two men left the dust of Pine Bluffs behind them and headed for Greeley.

Late the following afternoon they were pleased to find a town in marked contrast to Pine Bluffs for it meant a bed for at least one night, comfort away from the cold mountain nights.

The main street of Greeley bustled with activity. The storekeeper cajoled hands, specially hired to unload the wagon of supplies just in from Denver. Passengers said goodbye to relatives and friends in front of the stage office before boarding the stage drawn by six horses. A row of horses, hitched to the rail outside the saloon, switched their tails at the pestering flies. The batwings were in constant motion as men went to slake their thirst or emerged to go about their business. Housewives crossed the rutted road and avoided the horsemen and wagons which made the street a river of motion.

Outside the sheriff's office, two men, with stars pinned to their shirts, relaxed, deceivingly uninterested in the scene, but Red and Clem knew that nothing would miss their lazy gaze.

The two horsemen rode casually, figuring to be as inconspicuous as possible and reckoning that news of the gaolbreak back in Wyoming would be of no interest to the lawmen in Colorado. They pulled to a halt in front of the saloon, swung from the saddles and hitched their horses to the rail. They mounted the steps on to the sidewalk and sent the batwings squeaking once again.

They threaded their way between the tables, all occupied, to the mahogany, fancy carved counter which stretched the length of the wall opposite the entrance. Three barmen were busy keeping pace with customers' demands and saloon girls served the drinks to the men at the tables with whom they attempted to make a liaison with the promise of an exciting time.

As two foaming glasses of beer were pushed towards him, Clem held on to the coins when the barman reached out for them. Annoyance flicked the barman's face but he tempered it when he saw the hard light in Clem's eyes.

'Looking for a hombre name of Conroe,' said Red.

The barman hesitated. His eyes flashed from Clem to Red and back again.

'It's all right,' Clem put in quickly, his features softening, for he realized the barman knew Wes and he did not want to raise any suspicions. 'We know him from way back, punched cows together. Heard he'd settled in Greeley. Passing through, thought we'd look him up.'

The barman nodded. 'Sure thing. End of the main street, west, last house, right hand side. Runs the livery stable, down the street aways, on the left.'

'Thanks.' Clem released the money and turned to Red who had already downed half the beer.

The relief in Red's eyes changed to surprise, as he wiped his hand across his damp lips, 'Livery stable? Didn't know Wes was fond of horses. Must be going straight.'

'We'll have to persuade him different,' returned Clem raising his glass to his lips. He downed his beer. 'Let's go.'

'Hold it,' said Red. 'I want another. Wes ain't going away.'

'We get him lined up, then you can have all the beer you want.' Clem turned away and headed for the batwings.

Red's lips tightened in annoyance but he followed without another word.

The two men unhitched their horses and led

them down the street to the large wooden building announcing its purpose in letters painted above the double doors which were wide open.

A figure, rubbing a horse down at the far end of the stable, paused when he was aware of the break in the light as Clem and Red, with their horses, entered the building. Silhouetted as they were, he could not make out their features and saw them only as potential customers. He hurried to meet the newcomers who had stopped.

'G'day, gents. Want stabling?' he greeted as he approached them. 'You'll get good ...' His voice drained away. His stride had brought him within recognizable range. Focused on the man on the left, his eyes widened with astonishment and disbelief. 'Red!' The word came as a gasped whisper. 'What ...?'

'Seen a ghost, Wes?' grinned Red.

'Could be,' spluttered Wes. 'Didn't expect ...'

'Course, you didn't,' Red chuckled deep in his throat. 'Figured I'd still be in the pen?'

Wes shot a guarded glance at Clem and followed it with a querying look at his brother. 'Well, what would you think?' Wes was regaining his composure. 'How come you're here?'

'That's a long story, Wes Collins, or should I say Wes Conroe?' drawled Red.

Wes's lips tightened. So Red knew about his changed identity? He was on his guard; his suspicions roused. 'What d'you want?' he snapped.

Red grinned. 'A little matter of some cash, but that ain't the main reason.' Wanting to torment his brother's curiosity, Red turned his words. 'Oh, this here's Clem Adams.'

'Hi,' Clem held out his hand.

Wes nodded as he felt a friendly grip.

'Look after our horses while we book in at the hotel,' Red paused, shot his brother a mischievous look and said, 'unless you're going to invite us to stay with you?'

'Well, that ... er ... ain't possible,' stammered Wes, caught off his guard.

'You mean Kate wouldn't like it,' grinned Red.

'Yeah, you're dead right.' Wes stiffened. His eyes flashed with cold steel. 'I found her in Pine Bluffs. We married when we got here, kept her name, so don't you go upsetting things. I'll see you get your money then git.'

Red spread his arms wide. 'Now that ain't brotherly love, is it Clem? I said there was something more important than the money.'

'That sounds mighty suspicious coming from you.' Wes's eyes narrowed. 'What do you want here?'

'All in good time,' smiled Red. 'Here, take the horses.' He tossed his reins to Wes. 'We'll be back.'

Clem handed his reins to Wes, taking one last hard look at him as he did so. He saw a man a little taller than his brother, well built, with a face a little leaner than Red's. The eyes were sharp and clear and Clem knew instantly that Wes was a man alert to everything, a man guarded in his dealings. He knew it was not going to be easy to persuade him to return to Wyoming to do a job for Matt Palmer. Wes was settled, running his own livery stable, obviously accepted as one of the community, who knew nothing of his past. Here was a man who, after his crimes, had been able to go straight, had found his girl and settled down. He sure wasn't going to be easy to talk into upsetting his life. And, Clem figured, sympathy for his brother wouldn't run high. He'd play straight by him but maybe no more than that. However there might be a chance – blood is thicker than water.

'When you want 'em again?' asked Wes.

'Couple of days maybe, who knows?' Red shrugged his shoulders. 'Could depend on you.'

'Me?'

Red ignored his brother's query and turned to Clem. 'C'm on, Clem, let's find us a bed.' As he started for the street he called over his shoulder, 'We'll be back, Wes.' He edged his laugh with a touch of mystery.

Wes, his mind awhirl with the unexpected arrival of his brother, led the horses to their stalls. Red must have busted out of gaol, and that didn't auger well if he hung around Greeley. He had said a couple of days but it depended on him. He'd give the money, get rid of him but he'd hinted the money wasn't important. So why was he here? And who was this Clem? He hadn't said much but Wes was aware that he had been under close scrutiny from Clem. He didn't seem the rough-neck type he'd have expected Red to ride with. Wes was puzzled. He didn't like the situation. He didn't want his peace, his work or his marriage disturbing. His lips tightened. If Red upset Kate he'd kill him.

Wes and Clem crossed the street and strolled along the sidewalk in the direction of the hotel getting only casual glances from some of the cowboys and housewives who passed by.

A young woman hurried towards them. Her rapid steps beat a tattoo in marked contrast to measured stride of the two men. Her head slightly bowed, she seemed preoccupied with her thoughts.

Clem moved to one side to let her pass between them. Red altered his stride and took up the space, drawing a sharp look of annoyance from Clem. Suddenly aware that her path was blocked, the young woman swerved to pass Red, but he stepped in front of her. Her footsteps faltered and she glanced up.

'Howdy, Kate.' Red, amused by Kate's reaction, grinned down at her.

'Red!' Her gasp held disbelief as her annoyed expression changed to one of shock.

'Seen a ghost?' chuckled Red.

'How come you ...?' Kate's glance darted to Clem

and back again. In that moment she gathered her composure and, though her eyes still betrayed her shock, her thoughts were grasping at the situation created by the presence of her husband's brother. 'I thought we'd seen the last of you. What are you doing here?'

'You hoped you wouldn't see me again,' Red's voice went ice-cold and his eyes darkened. 'Expected me to rot in gaol while you enjoyed the money.'

'Money! That's why you're here. You want your share. Well you can have it all. We haven't touched a cent.'

Red laughed with disdain. 'Expect me to believe that. You'd need cash to buy yon livery stable.'

'You've seen Wes?' Kate's cry held dismay.

'Sure, I wanted to see my brother,' mocked Red.

'Don't give me that,' snapped Kate. 'You didn't come here out of brotherly love.' Her eyes flared and her lips tightened. 'Oh, just take the money and go; leave us alone; don't upset our lives.' She stepped past the two men and strode away with a determined step.

Red chuckled wryly. He glanced at Clem and caught a frown of annoyance. 'She could be trouble in persuading your brother to come with us.'

'She won't be, I'll see to that,' hissed Red. 'I ain't going back to that hell-hole because of her.'

As the two men started towards the hotel, Red glanced back and smiled to himself when he saw

Kate crossing the road towards the livery stable.

'Clem.' Red paused in his stride. 'If she's right and they didn't use that money, we can take it and to hell with Palmer and his schemes. You and I …'

'Forget it,' snapped Clem, his eyes cold with a steel-like warning. 'No one runs out on Palmer and gets away with it. We'd be looking over our shoulders at every step. He'd put Walt, Cadiz and Dex after us and you ain't seen Walt use that knife – I have and it ain't pleasant if you're on the receiving end. Now, let's get that room.' He strode off leaving Red pondering on his words.

'Wes!' Kate's call as she entered the stable brought her husband out of one of the stalls in the middle of the stable. Concern marked his face for he recognized anxiety in Kate's tone. 'You've seen him. I thought he'd still be in gaol. What's he want? Give him the money and send him packing.' The problem was quickly solved in the torrent of words.

'Hold on, lass. Don't take on so.' Wes's intonation offered comfort, as he took her arm with a reassuring grip, but Kate ignored the consolation.

'How can you be so calm with him here?' snapped Kate, irritated by Wes's seemingly off-hand manner.

'It's no good getting het up,' replied Wes quietly. 'He's here and we can't alter that. Like you, I thought he'd still be in gaol. I don't know how he comes to be out. And I am concerned. I don't want

53

our life upsetting.'

'Then get rid of him. Give him the money and let him go.' There was a desperate note in Kate's voice. She'd do anything to preserve the life she and Wes had built together. 'He didn't seem to believe me when I told him we hadn't touched the money.'

'You told him,' gasped Wes.

'It slipped out when I thought that was what he had come for. I'm sorry if I shouldn't …'

'It doesn't matter.' Wes waved away her apology. 'He'd have to know.'

'Let him take the lot,' urged Kate. 'We said we'd never touch it.'

'I know, love,' Wes frowned. 'I'd hoped to get rid of it to the right hands one day, but now, if Red takes it and flashes it around the authorities might start looking into the robbery again.'

Kate bit her lips. Wes had helped his brother in that robbery as one last throw for cash so that he could find Kate and set them up for life. He had found her but she had refused to marry him unless he promised to get rid of the money. Her persuasive powers had been strong and he had hidden the money in a safe place. Wes got work at Jake Bell's livery stable. Jake, getting on in years, liked the hard-working young fella, and, with no family of his own, had seen that when he died the stable, lock, stock and barrel, went to Wes. Wes now handled a thriving business, growing with the town's expansion. Nothing must upset the life which had become good for him.

'I don't think it's going to be as easy as giving him the money,' said Wes guardedly.

'What do you mean?' Alarm had sprung to Kate's eyes.

'Red hinted at some other reason for being here.'

'What?'

'I don't know. He said he'd be back.'

'Bring him to the house, Wes,' said Kate firmly. 'I want to hear what's going on.'

'Might be better if you don't get involved, love,' suggested Wes cautiously.

'Bring him home.' Wes knew from the strong tone in his wife's voice that she would brook no refusal.

'Both of them?' queried Wes.

'If it has to be, it has to be,' replied Kate. 'Know of this other fella?'

'No, never set eyes on him before,' said Wes.

'No doubt we'll find out.' Kate eyed her husband for a moment. 'You finished here?'

'Can do,' answered Wes.

'Then let's go home. I want nothing happening here that I don't know about. I don't trust that brother of yours.'

FIVE

'Guess Wes must have gone home,' observed Red, noting the doors closed on the livery stable.

'That means the little lady'll be at home,' said Clem.

'I told you, there'll be no trouble there,' answered Red.

Clem made no comment, but he was far from reassured by their meeting with Kate.

The two men headed for the house near the quieter edge of town. They passed the church, newly built, its white paintwork bright in the late sunlight. A row of board houses, each standing on its own plot of land, reflected the town's growing trade. Their neat gardens, with lilac bushes, blooming purple in the shade, complemented the brightly painted clapboards and veranda rails.

This end of town was in contrast to that which Red and Clem had seen on their arrival. There the majority of the gardens needed willing hands and determination to lick them into shape and the

57

woodwork on the houses needed some repair before receiving a coat of paint.

Red smiled to himself as he thought of the change in his brother; a bank robber, an expert with dynamite, now a respectable citizen running a livery stable under an assumed name, and living at the nob end of town. Well, that brother was in for a shock.

As they neared the end house, Red saw his brother sitting on the veranda. 'Waiting for us?' he called as he pushed open the gate in the fence.

He and Clem walked up the path between the trimmed edges of the lawn. Wes pushed himself from his chair and moved to the top of the four steps which came on to the veranda. His eyes bore no welcome for he had a feeling that Red's presence in Greeley did not auger well for him.

'Howdy, Mr Conroe, it's good to be here.' There was mockery in Red's tone as he put a special emphasis on the name.

'That's the name and you see it stays that way,' replied Wes coldly. 'You too,' he added shooting a warning glance at Clem.

'You've a right to the way you want it,' drawled Clem.

As Red and Clem mounted the steps, the door to the house swung open and Kate hurried out.

'Say what you have to say Red Collins and then get out of Greeley.' The fire in Kate's voice matched the hostility in her eyes.

'Collins? Collins?' grinned Red. 'I'm surprised you use that name around here Kate; folks might hear, and who knows what they'd think?'

Kate's lips tightened. She was annoyed with herself for using the name she had sworn never to use again when she married Wes. He was agreeable and they both wanted it that way, wanted the anonymity, and the settled life that went with it.

'Say what you want and get out of here,' she snapped.

'I'd like a word with you, Wes,' said Red, with a marked indication that he did not want Kate there.

'You'll say what you have to say in front of me,' rapped Kate sharply. 'If it concerns Wes it concerns me.'

'She's right, Red.' Wes added his agreement firmly as he moved beside his wife.

Red licked his lips in exasperation. He glanced at Clem whose nod gave his approval to Red to talk in front of Kate.

The exchange was not lost on Wes who concluded, with a curious interest, that Clem held some authority over Red.

'If it's the money he wants, give it to him, Wes,' said Kate with a glance at her husband.

Clem, seeing Red hesitate at the mention of the money, put in quickly, 'It isn't the money, ma'am, Red has another proposition.'

'I don't want to hear it,' replied Wes. 'It can't be good if it's coming from him.' Wes's thoughts were racing. Once again Clem showed authority. If the money wasn't of interest, and Wes couldn't believe that Red was really forgetting it, then there must be something bigger afoot. It must be on the wrong side of the law if Red was involved. His brother had always bucked authority since his early teens and had brushed with the law on more than one occasion. Wes had got involved with him once and Red held it over him forcing him to help him at other times. Then he had met Kate Conroe. He wanted to throw off the life Red had imposed on him but his older brother wouldn't let him. With Red's capture after their last bank robbery, Wes saw his opportunity, sought out Kate and persuaded her that crime was a thing of the past. Now he was not going to let anything spoil their settled life in Greeley.

'I think you'd better hear him out,' advised Clem. 'It could be good for you.'

'Nothing could be good for me coming from him,' cut in Wes sharply.

'Not only that,' Clem went on, ignoring Wes's remark, 'but you'll be doing him a favour.'

Wes gave a mock laugh. 'Why should I do him a favour, he ain't ever done me one? All he's brought is trouble.'

'Come on,' rapped Red, 'Ain't I set you up here, livery stable and all?'

'I told you we didn't use the money,' snapped Kate.

Seeing the look of disbelief on his brother's face, Wes added weight to Kate's statement.

'Never touched it, Red. Livery stable was left to us. And that's the truth. I don't owe you.'

'If you don't want to see Red rot in gaol, you'd better listen.' Clem's voice was low but his words were sharp and precise, compelling attention.

'Gaol, I figure that's where you should still be, so how come you're here?' asked Wes cautiously.

'Friends got him out,' replied Clem.

'Busted him out, you mean,' suggested Wes.

'Have it how you will, he's here now,' said Clem laconically.

'You one of those friends?' asked Wes.

'Manner of speaking. But reckon my boss is his real friend.'

'Who's he?' queried Wes.

'Matt Palmer.'

'Never heard of him.'

'You will.'

'Unlikely, if it's anything to do with him,' said Wes nodding at his brother.

'You got to, Wes,' called Red. 'Palmer got me out of gaol to find you.'

'Me? Why me?'

'You're good with dynamite.'

Immediately Wes was suspicious and from Kate's tightening grip on his arm he knew she was alarmed.

'Not any more,' he said. 'Those days are past.'

61

'They needn't be,' said Clem.

'This job Palmer wants me for, it can't be on the right side of the law if he was prepared to bust Red out of gaol to find me.' Wes's eyes narrowed with caution.

'Don't know what the job is,' replied Clem. 'But if the boss needs you it's important.'

'And if I refuse?' queried Wes.

'You'd miss a good pay out. Matt Palmer's generous.'

'And you'd be condemning me to that damned hell-hole I've been in,' cut in Red quickly.

'You mean he'd turn you back to the law,' said Wes.

'Sure, that's what he said,' urged Red.

'Would he?' Wes threw his question at Clem.

Clem nodded. 'Sure would.'

'You can't let him!' cried Red. 'It's worse than ...'

'Can't I?' cut in Wes contemptuously.

'Hell, no!' stormed Red. 'We're brothers!'

'Is that what Palmer reckoned on, brotherly love?' There was a half laugh in Wes's voice.

'Guess so,' returned Clem.

'Sure, he did. You must go along with him,' pleaded Red.

'Why should I?'

'For Ma's sake.' Red aimed at a weak spot. He knew Wes had been her favourite and that Wes would do anything for his mother. 'She'd want us to stick together, like she said on her deathbed.'

Wes's lips tightened at the memory. Pain came into his eyes. Kate sensed his tension tighten. She gripped his arm firmly, willing him not to weaken his resolve. Wes felt her fear. He patted her hand reassuringly.

'Ma wouldn't have wanted you in gaol in the first place,' rapped Wes coldly.

'And she wouldn't want to have me rotting there now, and that's what'll happen if I can't persuade you to come and see Palmer.'

'Where is he?'

Not sure what he should say, Red glanced at Clem.

'Wyoming,' replied Clem, who saw no reason to keep the information from Wes. 'Near a place called Creston. Far enough away not to affect you here.'

'Maybe, but it'll put me in Palmer's hands for evermore,' Wes pointed out. 'And I won't be beholden to any man.'

'Matt Palmer's not like that. One job and that's it as far as you're concerned,' returned Clem.

'So you say,' said Wes.

'Wes, you gotta help me,' pressed Red.

Wes stared at his brother.

'You will, you must,' urged Red. 'I can't go back to that hell-hole and it'll be worse if the law gets me again. This one job for me, Wes, and then I'll be far gone where no one will ever find me, out of your lives forever.'

Clem, seeing a weakening in Wes's resolve, deemed it wise to let him think things over. 'You've two days, to decide. We must leave Greeley then. Maybe you'd better decide to come with us, not only for your brother's sake but for your own. The folks of Greeley might not take too well to knowing that Wes Conroe, their livery stable man, is really Wes Collins, wanted for bank robbery!'

SIX

'Wes, what are we going to do?' cried Kate when the two horsemen were out of earshot. The anguish in her eyes tore at Wes's heart.

Why the hell had Red come back into their lives? Wes's lips tightened at the thought of what it meant. Damn this Palmer who had the gall and the influence to bust a man out of a gaol noted for its high security. 'Damn, damn, damn.' Wes pounded his fist into his hand. 'Why the hell did they come for me? Blast the day I got mixed up with dynamite.' When he turned to his wife and reached out to take her into his arms, sorrow and regret mingled in his eyes. 'I'm sorry, love, I've brought you trouble again.'

Kate buried her head in his shoulder. 'What can we do?' she sobbed.

'What's best to keep our way of life,' he soothed. Then a note of determination crept into his voice. 'Nobody's going to spoil that.'

Kate eased herself away from him and looked at

him with troubled eyes. 'But they'll tell the folks who you really are.'

'Not if I stop them.' Wes's first thought was to buckle on the gun he had not worn for five years.

Kate sensed his intention. 'No! You can't!' she cried. 'That will only make things worse. You could get killed or be branded a killer.' The concern and pleading in Kate's eyes jolted Wes and cleared his mind.

'You're right, love, that's no answer.' He released his hold on her and leaned despairingly on the veranda rail. 'Seems there's only one thing to do, play along with them. Get the job done, whatever it is, and get back here.'

'But it must be on the wrong side of the law,' cried Kate. 'I know we said that when the right opportunity arose, we'd return the money from the last bank robbery but couldn't we use it to get rid of these two?'

'If Red had been on his own that might have worked, but this here Clem's a different proposition. I reckon he's Palmer's sidekick sent along to see that Red don't run out on him. He ain't interested in the money.'

'Give it to Red and persuade him to run out on Clem,' suggested Kate.

Wes straightened and grasped his chin thoughtfully. 'But if Red agreed, Clem still knows where I am and it appears that I'm the one Palmer wants. Seems to me the only solution is to go along with them.'

'But that'll put you on the wrong side of the law and if things go wrong ...' Kate shuddered and her eyes filled with tears.

Wes took her into the comfort of his arms. 'Nothing will go wrong, love. I'll make sure of that.'

With her head against his chest she could not see the concern which clouded his face, nor his lips tightening in a resolve to try to scupper this unwanted affair before it began.

He pushed her gently from him. 'Wipe those tears away, love. We'll work something out. Now, you get our meal ready while I slip back to the stable, there's something I forgot to do.' He smiled reassuringly at her.

Kate swallowed hard and smiled wanly at her husband. 'Sorry, Wes, I should have more strength.'

'No, love. You've had a shock. It was like a ghost appearing.' He kissed her on the forehead. 'You get that food ready, I shan't be long.'

Wes turned away, stepped from the veranda and hurried to the stable. He opened the small door and stepped inside. His determined stride took him to the ladder leading to the hay loft at the far end of the stable. He climbed quickly and scattered hay until he reached a wooden box half hidden against the wall.

The hinges creaked as he raised the lid. He stared at the contents, hesitating while his brain whirled conflicting thoughts around in his mind. Was this the answer? Was this the only thing he could do? Would it enable him to preserve the stable life he and Kate had carved out in Greeley? Kate! He'd do anything to protect her from trouble, but was this the way?

He reached down slowly and picked up the gunbelt, holster and Colt. Memories came pouring back as he weighed the gun in his hand. His father had shown him and Red how to use a gun under the philosophy of you never know when you might need it but use it only in self-defence. The brothers had practised until they were both good shots. With Wes always keeping his pa's words in mind, he was troubled by the mean gleam which came into Red's eyes whenever he held a Colt. He sensed there would be trouble, for he read in those eyes a desire to use the weapon for his own ends. One day, Red had stepped on to the wrong side of the law and, eventually had taken a reluctant Wes with him until the final raid went wrong and Red had been brought down in the get-away.

When Wes had come to Greeley he had hidden the Colt swearing to Kate and to himself that he would never wear it again.

Wes let the lid close slowly. He stared at the gun for a moment longer, then, a decision made, he strapped the belt quickly around his waist. He checked it for comfort, then tied the leather throng around his thigh holding the holster firmly in place. He checked the hang of the gun and made a final adjustment. It felt as if it had never been absent from his waist.

He tensed himself. No! Relax. Wes drove the tension from his body. He needed to be sharp, alert but in a relaxed way. Tension must not hamper his actions. His hand, swift to the butt of his Colt, drew the weapon in one clean movement. But Wes was not satisfied. The gun had not cleared leather as smoothly as it used to. He slipped it back into the holster. He went through the motion again, shook his head and tried again. It was only after a dozen draws that he felt his old skill returning. After six more tries he straightened with a self-satisfied pleasure suffusing his body. He had not lost the ability to make a fast draw.

Wes climbed down the ladder, crossed the stable, stepped outside, locked the door and set off in the direction of the hotel.

As he crossed the road and clattered along the sidewalk, he was aware of several glances cast in his direction. Wes Conroe wearing a gun; never seen him with one before; what's wrong? He could sense what people were thinking.

There was no one in the lobby when he entered the hotel. The clerk rose to his feet from the chair behind the desk.

'Howdy, Wes.' The man was curious. He couldn't recall Wes coming into the hotel before.

'Jake.' Wes nodded. 'Couple of strangers booked

in here short while ago. Where can I find them? Want to know when they want their horses.'

'Short one's in room seven, taller of the two's ...' Jake's voice faded. Wes was already at the foot of the stairs. He had heard all he wanted to know.

Jake stared, his eyes widening with surprise. He started to call out but let the words freeze on his lips. It was no concern of his, but Wes Conroe was wearing a gun. Should he get the sheriff? He had no one to send. He started round the desk. No, he couldn't leave the hotel. Maybe he would be better here if there was trouble. But why should there be? He was jumping to conclusions. It was the surprise at seeing Wes wearing a gun. He wasn't a man prone to anger. He always presented a mild, peace-loving side. Besides, any man was entitled to wear a gun so why not Wes? But these were strangers in town. Had they any connection with Wes which had necessitated him strapping on a Colt? The clerk shrugged his shoulders and sat down. Who was he to worry? It was no concern of his. He picked up his paper but his curiosity had been roused. He did not see the words for he was concentrating on trying to identify sounds from above.

He heard Wes's footsteps go along the corridor. They stopped. He heard a door open and shut and guessed that Wes had entered room seven. How he wished he was a fly on the wall.

If he had been he would have seen the look of

surprise cross Red's face when Wes stepped into the room.

'Oh, little brother's wearing a gun.' Red's voice held mockery as he swung from a lying position to sit on the edge of the bed. 'Come to ride with us?'

'I want you out, away from here,' rapped Wes coldly.

Red grinned. 'You figure that'll do it.' He nodded at the weapon.

'If it has to.'

Red shook his head. 'It won't. You'll never use it. You never could and never will. If you'd had the guts to squeeze the trigger you could have dropped Sheriff Millett and saved me from that hell-hole of a gaol.' Red shook his head slowly. 'No, you'll never use it.'

'It'll persuade you to leave,' snapped Wes, taken aback when Red's assessment of the truth bit deep into his mind.

'Wouldn't do you any good,' drawled Red. 'If I ran out on Palmer, his men would get me and they'd get you now they know where you are.'

Wes's lips tightened. Red was right. 'Look, take all the money from the last raid. You and Clem, split it between you. Tell Palmer you can't find me, or better still disappear where he can't find you.' A desperate note had come to Wes's voice.

'You don't know Palmer and you sure don't know Clem, he's loyal. And I ain't going back to gaol.' Red's tone firmed with certainty. 'You're coming with us and if anyone's using a gun it'll be me to make certain you do.'

'Red's right.'

Wes started. He had not heard the door open. Clem stood with his back to the closed door and held a gun pointing straight at Wes.

'Like I said,' Clem went on quietly, 'the folk of Greeley wouldn't take kindly to knowing who Wes Conroe really is. We leave in the morning. Be ready.' Clem stepped away from the door, an indication that there was nothing more to be said.

Wes knew it was useless. His glare was met with a mocking grin from his brother and a non-committal coldness from Clem. Wes, curbing his temper, jerked the door open and stormed down the corridor.

The clerk's query of 'Find 'em, Wes?' was ignored as Wes strode across the lobby and slammed out of the hotel.

'Wes!' Kate stared in horror at the gunbelt around his waist. 'You said you'd never wear that again. It ain't the answer.'

Wes unbuckled the belt and dropped it in a chair. 'I thought it might be. I went intending to run them out of town but it was no use. If I'd used it our life here would have been ruined. I offered them all the money but Clem's not interested. The only way is to go with them. If I do, I might be able to preserve our life here.'

SEVEN

'Goodbye, love.' Wes took Kate in his arms. His kiss was long as if he needed to impress it deep in his heart.

'Take care, Wes.' Tears stung her eyes as Kate fought to hold them back. She had sworn not to let Wes see her cry. 'Come back soon.' The words clung in her throat.

'I will.' He stepped back and her arms slipped helplessly to her sides. With one last look which imprinted her attractive beauty indelibly in his memory, Wes turned and swung into the saddle. He tapped his horse and sent it out of town.

Kate watched until he passed out of sight. Sadness and fear mingled as she walked back into the house. As the door close behind her she leaned back against it. She hugged herself, her arms crossed tightly below her breasts, trying to stifle the sobs which raked her body. Now she let the tears flow.

The peaceful life, she and Wes had built here in

73

Greeley could be lost forever. She feared the worst, for, unknown to Wes, she had seen him store his Colt and gunbelt in his saddlebag.

Five miles north of Greeley, at a fork in the trail, Wes slowed his horse. He had expected Red and Clem to be waiting. He had insisted that they left Greeley separately. The less the townfolk linked him with the two strangers the better. He stopped and reached in his saddlebag for his Colt.

He turned his mount. With narrowed gaze he surveyed his immediate surroundings from beneath the brim of his stetson, tipped forward to shield his eyes from the glare beating from the clear sky and thrown back by the parched ground. The landscape was still and nothing stirred among the group of boulders a hundred yards to his right.

He angled his horse towards them. Their slightly elevated position would give him a good sight of the country towards Greeley and maybe he could find some shade. Reaching them he slipped from the saddle and made sure his horse was as comfortable as possible in the shadow of the biggest boulder before he found himself a vantage point, hidden from view, from which he could see the trail.

He fastened his gun-belt around him and adjusted it so that the butt of the Colt lay naturally to the drop of his hand.

He smiled to himself as he settled. All the old

habits were back. Positioning his gun, weighing situations carefully, making sure he had every possible advantage, and caution, all were there as if they had never left him and had been employed every day. They had paid off in the past whereas Red's impetuosity had been his undoing on more than one occasion.

He slipped the stetson from his head, wiped the sweat from his forehead and eased himself more comfortably among the boulders. Red and Clem were late. His mind wandered. Who was this fella Matt Palmer and what did he want dynamite for? He wished he'd never got a reputation for being good with explosives. Then maybe he'd still be tending horses in Greeley. Whatever it was that Palmer had in mind it must be big for him to go to the trouble of busting Red out of gaol in order to find himself. And if it was big then there'd be risks and he didn't want anything which would put him too near the law.

He started. A dust cloud broke the distant flatness. Riders. The disturbance set Wes's mind racing. If he got his rifle he could drop these two, hide the bodies and return to his life in Greeley.

He half rose and then sank back with a curse. Palmer no doubt knew where Red would start looking and if Red had found him then couldn't Palmer's sidekicks do the same? Hadn't Clem hinted at that? He'd have to leave Greeley and if he did he'd always be looking over his shoulder. That wouldn't be fair to Kate. They'd never be able to settle. They'd never know the peace they had in Greeley. No, there was only one way, get this job over and get out. Risks there'd be but he'd minimize those as much as he could by running things his way. He had what Palmer wanted and he could dictate, but above all he'd have to curb the impetuosity of his brother.

He watched the two riders draw nearer and nearer. When they were within hailing distance he stood up. The movement and his shout brought the two men hauling their horses to a halt. Then they turned them in his direction and a few minutes later he was greeting them as he scrambled down the boulders.

'Expected you'd be here before me.'

'Had to drag this brother of yours out of the whore-house,' explained Clem with a look of annoyance in which Wes also noted disapproval.

Red grinned. 'You fellas ain't been penned up in gaol. Gotta make up for lost time.'

Clem looked hard at Red. 'All right, but from now on you keep your mind on Matt Palmer's job.'

Red shrugged his shoulders. 'How can I when I don't know what it is?'

'You'll know when he wants you to know. In the meantime you do nothing which will jeopardize that job. So walk carefully.' His eyes narrowed. 'Hell, those girls ain't above passing information to the law if it suits their ends. And ease off the drink, that can make you talk.'

Red stiffened, annoyed at Clem's attitude. 'Damn you, you ain't running my life.'

'While you're working for Palmer I am,' snapped Clem leaving Red in no doubt about the consequences should he step out of line.

Red turned his attention to his brother. 'See you're still wearing that pea-shooter. Ain't you frightened it might go off?' he mocked.

Wes's lips tightened. He knew Clem's eyes were on him, wondering how he would handle the situation and ready to judge him in the way he did.

But before he could answer, Red went on. 'D'you know, Clem, if he'd pulled the trigger on Sheriff Millet he'd have saved me going to gaol.'

'And if I had,' rapped Wes, 'we'd both probably have hanged.'

'You got away and I rotted in gaol,' hissed Red, with a venom which showed that he still condemned his brother.

'You'd only yourself to blame,' rapped Wes. 'If you hadn't been so greedy we'd have both got away. If you hadn't turned back for that extra bag of money, Sheriff Millet wouldn't have got that shot at you.' His face darkened and there was danger in the cold steel of his voice. 'Now, get off my back, brother, or I'll pull out of this one and see you back in gaol.'

'Why you …' Red started to go for his Colt.

'Stow it!' rapped Clem swinging his horse against

Red's and throwing him off balance so that his hand never closed on the butt. He glared angrily at Red. 'Cut this out, both of you.' Though he included Wes in his remarks, they were clearly aimed at Red whom he saw as the trouble-maker and one on whom he would have to keep a special watch. 'The past is gone. All we're concerned about now is getting Matt Palmer's job done. And don't you forget it. Any more trouble, Red, and you won't know what's hit you. Now, let's ride.'

He turned his horse. Wes, ignoring his brother, swung into the saddle and set the animal after Clem. A moment later he heard the clatter of hooves behind him.

Three men headed to a destiny in Wyoming.

EIGHT

Clem halted his horse at the top of the rise. Wes and Red stopped beside him.

'Palmer's place,' Red informed his brother.

Surprise marked Wes's face as he glanced at Clem for confirmation. This was not at all what he had expected. About two miles away, in a fertile river valley, lay a working ranch, nestling in a curve of the hill. A long, low, ranch house, stables, a bunkhouse, corrals – there was every hallmark of respectability. Two men emerged from the stable and hurried to join others who were at the corrals working with what Wes judged to be unbroken horses. Wes shook his head in incredulity. He had expected to be taken to some hideout, some out-of-the-way place, a robber's roost, not a reputable ranch. But then many things in this life are not what they seem. Take himself. Who, in Greeley, would have associated the owner of their livery stable with a bank robber, an expert with dynamite?

'Let's meet the boss,' Clem broke into Wes's thoughts.

The three men put their mounts down the slope and by the time they reached the house word had passed in to Matt Palmer who now stood on the veranda.

Wes knew he was being observed critically by a man whom he figured went a lot on first impressions. For his own part he figured he would be dealing with a man who knew exactly what he wanted and who would stand no nonsense to get it. There was authority in his very stance and he knew he was observing a man who expected to be obeyed without question, but he also figured that he was a man who would be fair and would not forget loyalty. And he reckoned from Palmer's build he was a man who would work alongside his men whenever the situation demanded it. But what did such a man require of him? What was it that made him prepared to bust the likes of Red out of jail just so he could make this contact?

'Howdy.' Palmer nodded his greeting. 'Glad your brother found you, Collins. Pleased to see you. Guess you'd like to wash off the dust.' He turned his gaze to Clem. 'Get him a bunk and then bring him over.'

Clem raised his hand in acknowledgement and turned his horse towards the bunkhouse.

Ten minutes later Clem rapped on the door of the ranch house and walked in, followed by Wes and Red, without waiting for an acknowledgement. Wes knew Clem carried a strong trust from Palmer. He was more than a mere top-hand, more than a trouble-shooter.

Wes noted the neat, tidy elegance as they crossed the hall to a door on the right. Clem tapped on the door and this time there was a slight hesitation before he opened it at the call of, 'Come.'

Palmer was sitting behind his mahogany desk and two chairs had been placed opposite to him. He stood up and held out his hand to Wes.

'Glad you came.'

Wes took his hand and felt strength in the fingers. 'Pleased to know you, Mr Palmer.' Wes kept his tone neutral.

Palmer turned his gaze on Red. 'I didn't ask you to come.'

'But I figured ...' Red started, his eyes flaring with surprise.

'You ain't got to figure, just stay strictly to what you're told,' rapped Palmer as he sat down.

'Look here,' snapped Red, 'I got you Wes.'

'Sure. You did what you were told.' Palmer's eyes smouldered beneath bushy eyebrows. 'Leave it that way.'

'You couldn't operate if I hadn't got him.' Red, grieved that Palmer was treating him as of no account, gritted his teeth.

'That don't entitle you to anything except payment,' snarled Palmer. 'Certainly you aren't privilege to what I'm going to say to your brother. Now, git.'

'But I reckon you owe me more …'

'I don't,' boomed Palmer straightening in his chair.

'Out,' rapped Clem, stepping in to the situation for the first time. He moved towards Red.

Red stood defiant.

Clem stopped, his face close to Red's. 'Another thing, town's out for you until Mr Palmer clears it. You're liable to throw your gab. Now, git.' His eyes bored deep into Red's.

For one moment Red's surging anger threatened to erupt, then suddenly he turned on his heel and strode from the room slamming the door as he went out.

'Sit down,' said Palmer indicating the two chairs. He eyed Wes. 'Sorry about that.' He paused, his eyes still riveted on Wes, then said, 'Didn't spring to your brother's defence.'

'That was his battle not mine,' replied Wes.

'You and he get on?' queried Palmer.

'Could say we do, could say we don't,' replied Wes lightly.

Matt pursed his lips then glanced at Clem. 'How'd they get on?'

'Well, I wouldn't say they got along like two pups in a basket,' replied Clem. 'In fact they were down-right ornery with each other at times.'

Palmer rubbed his chin. 'Well, that might be

awkward,' he commented. 'I figured brotherly love ...'

'Let's quit the cackling, Mr Palmer,' cut in Wes sharply. 'I know you want me for a job; you busted Red out of jail to find me and threatened to put him back there if he couldn't persuade me to come here. There may be no love lost between us but blood is thicker than water, I should hate him to go back to the hell-hole he described. Now, let's waste no more time. Tell me why I'm here and then let me get back to Greeley, to my wife and my livery stable.' Wes's voice had firmed with determination.

'I like a man who knows what he wants,' said Palmer, 'and gets ...'

'You going to get on with it or am I leaving?' rapped Wes.

Clem stiffened but Matt waved him to relax.

'All right, Wes. I need your expertise with dynamite.'

'Why me, Mr Palmer? There are others ...'

'Not as good as you,' broke in Matt. 'And cut out the Mr Palmer. It's Matt as long as you ride for me.'

Wes eyed Matt suspiciously. 'I don't ride for you. One job and one job only.'

'All right. All right,' Matt dismissed Wes's protest.

'And don't you forget it,' went on Wes, his voice like a thrust of steel. He drew confidence from the ace in his hand. He had a skill which Matt wanted so he could call the tune. 'Try for me again and I'll blow the lid off this one even if it means me going down with you.'

Matt eyed Wes. 'You would, wouldn't you?'

'Damned right I would. I'd carved out a peaceable life for myself; you've interrupted it. The sooner I get back to it and am left in peace the better.' He stared hard at Matt. He knew he was bucking authority but what the hell?

Matt did not answer for a moment. Then he leaned back in his chair and started to laugh. 'Wes Colllins, I like you. No one has spoken to me like that since my pa. Good for you. Right, I need you to blow a hole in an armoured coach.'

'Armoured coach?' Wes was puzzled.

'I know that $500,000 of government money is being shipped from Fort Phil Kearny to Cheyenne for shipment back east. It's being transported in a steel coach. That's what I want you to blow.'

'But, Matt, what about all this?' Wes indicated that he was referring to the ranch.

Matt laughed. 'A front, a cover, Wes. Yes I carry on a successful ranching business here; I'm respected in town. No one knows that Matt Palmer is the brains behind several big bank raids throughout the territory. I never work on my doorstep. Same as this one. The coach will be hit at Glenrock, over a hundred miles from here, the other side of the Laramie Mountains.'

'Won't it be heavily guarded?' queried Wes.

Matt smiled. 'That's what everyone would think.

But so as not to draw special attention to it there will be only six men with it and the authorities will put out that it's just the coach which is being moved to Cheyenne for a trip back east. It will not be heavily guarded at its night stops – maybe the authorities figure the steel is strong enough if anyone tries anything.'

'This place Glenrock?' asked Wes.

'Small town, little there and that's why I figure they're using it for a night stop. Insignificant place, won't draw attention to the coach.'

Wes nodded. He eyed Matt. 'How do you know your information is correct?'

Matt smiled. 'Money, Wes; money can get you any information you want.'

'Supposing we find the information is incorrect and that the coach has a heavily armed army escort?'

'Cautious, Wes. You've every right to be. If that turns out to be the situation then the whole thing is off. I'll not mix with the army. Clem knows that and he will be the judge in the field.' Matt leaned back in his chair and fixed Wes with his deep blue eyes. Now there was the cold steel of power in them. 'Go away and think about it.'

Wes shook his head. 'First the little matter of payment.'

'I wondered when you'd think of that,' said Matt. '$10,000.'

Wes met Matt's gaze and shook his head slowly.

Matt's eyes narrowed. '$15,000.'

Wes still shook his head slowly.

Matt straightened in his chair. 'Now look here, Collins.'

Wes continued to shake his head without speaking.

Matt's lips tightened. 'All right $20,000, but no more.'

A faint grin flicked Wes's lips as he continued to shake his head.

'Damn you!' Matt's face was beginning to redden with fury at this whipper-snapper who dared to bargain with him. '$25,000 and that's definitely the last word.'

Wes shook his head.

Matt turned to Clem, his eyes blazing in angry temper. 'Get him out of here. Out, I say.'

'Hold it, Clem,' said Wes, stopping Clem from rising. He looked back at Palmer. 'You need me, Matt,' he said quietly. 'But you ain't asked me how much I want.'

'$25,000, not a penny more,' fumed Matt.

'Ask me,' said Wes.

Matt's lips tightened. His eyes darkened. 'How much?' he hissed.

'Nothing!'

The momentary silence was charged with disbelief.

'Nothing?' Wide-eyed, Matt spat the word with mistrust.

'That's dead right,' replied Wes.

'But ...' Matt spluttered trying to find his words, 'you're turning the job down?'

Wes shook his head. 'No. I'll do the job. All I want in return is an assurance that you won't hand Red back to the authorities.'

'You got that,' replied Matt. 'But the $25,000 I've offered you?'

'Don't want it. It'd give you a hold over me. You'd press me into other jobs and I don't want that. I'll do this job for my brother.' Wes raised his eyes heavenwards. 'God knows why. He's a heap of trouble. He ain't done me a favour turning up like this but I reckon a brother's a brother and I wouldn't wish my worst enemy time in that damned prison.'

Matt shook his head slowly, still in disbelief that someone should turn down an offer of cash. 'Figure you got enough out of that hold-up you did with him,' he commented.

'Ain't touched that money. Should never have got involved with Red on that one. Built up my livery business without it. That cash is going back where it belongs when I get back to Greeley. Then I'm clean.'

Matt spread his arms in a gesture of resignation. 'All right, if that's the way you want it.'

'That's exactly how I want it,' Wes confirmed. 'When do we hit this coach?'

'A week's time. We'll discuss the details tomorrow.' Matt's statement acted as a dismissal and the two men left his company.

NINE

Two days later five men, Wes, Red, Walt, Dex and Cadiz led by Clem, headed along a trail which climbed through the mountains over the 6000ft pass at Muddy Gap, past Devil's Gate to pick up the Oregan Trail within sight of the massive landmark of Independence Rock. They passed Red Buttes, skirted Mills, Casper and Evansville, lazing under the hot Wyoming sun, and made camp in the hills overlooking Glenrock. They had a day to spare.

'I'm heading for town, anyone coming?' There was a note of keen anticipation of a night of drinking and women in Red's voice as he threw the coffee dregs from his tin mug across the parched earth. He started to push himself to his feet.

No one moved but five pairs of eyes viewed him with surprised doubt that his statement could be serious. One pair hardened into distrust.

'Hold it,' rapped Clem. 'No one goes anywhere until this job's over.'

'Hell, Clem, you ain't going to keep us on a tight

rein tonight and all tomorrow?' Red glared at the
man bossing the outfit.

Clem's eyes narrowed, never wavering under
Red's piercing look. 'I am. No one leaves this camp.
You try and you're in trouble. You could jeopardize
the whole set-up, so forget it.' Clem's nimble mind
was racing ahead to tomorrow. He realized he
would have to watch Red carefully or give him a job
which would tie him up. 'And don't get the idea of
giving Glenrock the once-over tomorrow. I've a job
for you.'

'What the hell's that?' snarled Red. 'I figured ...'

'You ain't paid to figure,' Clem cut in sharply.
'You just do as you're told.'

Cold steel flashing from Clem's eyes told Red it
was better to say no more. His lips tightened as he
slumped back against his bedroll and saddle.

The rest of the group, tense during this
exchange, relaxed again. Walt, Cadiz and Dex
anticipated the haul they would make; they knew
Palmer would be generous in his handout if they
pulled it off. Wes thought of Kate and the peaceful
life they had found in Greeley and cursed the events
which threatened to take it from him. Whatever
happened he was determined that he would return
to that life. He wanted no part of this raid but he was
cornered. Get it over, get away, back to Greeley and
forget the whole thing, return the money from the
bank robbery and see that his brother never stepped
into his life again.

* * *

Cadiz haunched close to the fire and drew on the sharp morning air as he stirred the embers into life. He placed some wood carefully so that it caught the heat reviving amongst the ash. As he watched the glow grow into life, his mind anticipated a day of idleness preparing for the moment when they would hit that steel wagon and leave Glenrock a lot richer.

'Quit mooning and git the coffee on,' ribbed Dex, crouching beside Cadiz.

Cadiz started then grinned at Dex. He grabbed the coffee pot, threw in some grains, filled it with water and thrust it on to the flames which were taking hold of the wood. Dex placed some bacon in a pan and in a matter of moments an appetising smell tinged the Wyoming air.

The camp stirred and within fifteen minutes the rest of the outfit were sampling Dex's frying. Friendly banter passed between them, though Wes tended to speak only when spoken to. Red, ignored by the others, remained morose. It was as if they did not regard him as one of them, as if he were an outsider being tolerated because he had been useful to their boss; his services had been used and now he was not really necessary to their plans. They did not like his loud, boastful manner nor the fact that he wanted to buck authority. In this they sensed he could be a danger to their mission.

It came as a relief to them when Clem, with the meal finished, dictated the plans for the day.

'Wes and I will give the town the once-over and lay plans for tonight. Red, I want you back along the trail now to watch for the wagon. Take some tack and water and only come in once you've sighted it.'

Red stiffened. 'Hell! It ain't due 'til late afternoon, time for us all to hit town.'

'No one goes to town but Wes and myself.' Clem's words were steel.

'Aye, you and Wes can have yourselves a good time.' Red looked at the others. 'You ain't standing for this, are you?'

Walt, Cadiz and Dex ignored his outburst.

'They know how we operate,' said Clem icily. 'The first thing is to obey orders. If we all go into town we'll draw too much attention. Drinking and womanizing – you are likely to blow things, so keep away from Glenrock. That's why I want you back along the trail.' He paused, then added, 'So don't go getting ideas about bucking my orders.'

Red's lips tightened. For one moment he glared defiantly at Clem, but Clem's fixed look turned him away. He grabbed his saddle and made for his horse.

Glenrock lay quiet under the heat of the early afternoon sun when two dust-covered riders eased their mounts slowly along the main street towards the saloon. They looked as if they had been in the saddle a long time and were just longing to get their lips at a cold beer. With dust covering their horses, the image was complete except that anyone taking a close look might have noticed that the animals did not seem all that weary, but in this heat, in a town which boasted fewer than two hundred inhabitants, there was no one about to notice.

Weary as the travellers looked, their eyes were alert, taking in the layout of the town, noting the position of the buildings and liking the fact that there was no sheriff's office.

'Where d'ya reckon they'll put the wagon for the night?' Wes kept his voice low.

'By the livery stable,' returned Clem. 'Handy for the horses and it's as good as anywhere in this place.'

Wes studied the livery stable and its surrounds as they rode past. The open ground behind the stable with low hills but a mile away would give them the best possible escape route. The explosion would attract immediate attention but Wes knew that Clem, who was also studying the same area, would have the get-away horses placed just right.

'Anything trouble you about the set-up here?' queried Clem as he swung his horse to the hitching-rail outside the saloon.

'No,' replied Wes.

'Then, let's get that drink.' Clem swung from his saddle.

Was followed suit in an easy, flowing movement.

They flicked the reins around the wood, noting that the only horse hitched to the rail bore signs of travel.

Clem and Wes strode on to the boardwalk and stepped towards the batwings of the saloon. From habit Clem paused and took in the room at a quick glance over the top of the batwings. Wes was beside him.

'Damn!' The word hissed low from Wes and at the same time he moved swiftly to one side turning with his back against the wall.

Clem shot Wes a surprised glance and, always alert for any untoward happening, he too, from force of habit moved with Wes. 'What's wrong?' he asked sharply.

'At the bar,' whispered Wes. 'Cap Millet, he was the sheriff who got Red when we hit the bank.'

'Damn.' Clem's teeth were clenched. 'He'd know you?'

'Sure,' replied Wes. 'What the hell's he doing here?'

Clem nodded to the horse. 'Maybe just passing through.' 'You go to the store. Buy something. I'l see what I can find out and see you in the store.'

Wes nodded and made off at a steady walk towards the store.

Clem pushed the batwings open and let them swing squeakily behind him. He strolled casually to the long counter studying Cap Millet as he weaved between the tables, only two of which were occupied. The saloon had the same sleepy air as the rest of the town.

Cap was hunched over the bar but Clem judged he would be tall and lean when he straightened. He sensed a power in the man, a power held back like a coiled spring ready to be unleashed whenever the necessity arose. Through the mirror behind the bar Clem saw Cap's face was burned brown from the lined forehead to the firm, clean shaven, square chin. He bore the marks of travel but there was no weariness about the eyes. They were alert, taking in everything.

'Beer, please,' said Clem as the pot-bellied barman moved to serve him.

He was aware of Millet studying him in a casual way through the mirror. He recognized the thoroughness of a man who was or had been an efficient lawman.

Clem met the look and nodded. 'Ridden far?' he asked.

'Some,' replied Millet. 'From Cheyenne. You're dust-covered too.'

'All the way from Pine Ridge,' lied Clem.

'Heading for?' asked Cap, as a matter of habit.

'Jeffrey City.'

'Pushing on today?'

'Reckon so.'

'I figure I've had enough for today and I ain't pushed.' Cap shot a glance at the bartender. 'That sick looking hotel any good?'

'It'll give you a bed, that's about saying how good it is.' The barman hesitated a moment as he eyed Cap. 'You look all right, not one to take advantage of a lady, so tell you what, you go to Widow Turner's. Third house from the east end. Blue door, white fence. She'll be home from home for you. Comfy, good food. Could do with the money.'

'Thanks.' Cap nodded. 'Home cooking I look forward to. Fed up of trail grub.' Cap drained his glass, straightened, glanced at Clem and with a 'Good riding,' left the saloon.

Clem waited a few minutes, toying with the last dregs in his glass, then drank them, nodded to the barman and strolled out on to the boardwalk. He paused, glancing both ways along the dry, sun-drenched street. It was still and silent as if it wanted nothing to do with the day and seemed to resent the only person who disturbed this attitude – Cap Millet whom Clem saw walking his horse towards the east end of town.

Clem now sent another ripple of movement to upset Glenrock's desired sleepiness as he headed for the store.

He found Wes examining some hats near one of the windows.

'He's come from Cheyenne. Didn't say where he was heading but he ain't pushed so he's staying the night.' Clem kept his voice low as he tried on a hat.

'Damn!' hissed Wes. 'That ain't good.'

Clem noticed the alarm in Wes's eyes. 'Don't

panic,' he whispered. 'Buy a hat and let's mosey out of here.'

Wes tried on a couple of hats, chose one, paid the storekeeper who, delighted to make a sale, fussed over the purchase. Wes curbed his impatience to be away, then, when the transaction was completed, the two men bade the storekeeper, 'Good day,' and strolled casually from the store.

Clem stepped on to the boardwalk first and quickly took in the scene. Cap had disappeared. When Clem made no sign Wes joined him without giving a hint of his hesitation. He need not have worried about being observed by the storekeeper for the thin, gaunt man was handling the notes he had just been given with delighted avarice.

The two men started to walk towards their horses.

'I ain't happy with Millet around,' said Wes.

'He'll be asleep tonight like everyone else,' replied Clem. 'We've got just the same opportunity, Millet or no Millet.'

Wes gave a half laugh. 'You ain't run up against him. Once that dynamite blows it'll be as if he was standing beside you.'

'No man's as fast as that,' commented Clem, a touch of derisory disbelief in his voice.

'Ain't he?' Wes answered.

'Then we'll just have to be that bit faster,' pointed out Clem.

TEN

Once again Red cursed the heat, cursed Clem Adams for condemning him to this useless vigil and cursed the inactivity when he could have been living it up in Glenrock.

Nothing had moved on the trail from the north all morning and it was no better in the early afternoon. Red shifted his position, trying to find a more comfortable place but that was nigh impossible on the hard rocks. He settled himself for – how many times? He couldn't have guessed. And each time raised irritation to anger point.

Even the antics of a little rock lizard which scudded on to the rock to his right and looked him over with a searching curiosity failed to amuse him. Each time it appeared he flipped pebbles at it, seeing it as Clem come to make sure he was maintaining his lookout.

He eased his battered stetson, wiped the beads of sweat from his forehead, and tipped the hat back on his head. Then he took a swig from his water bottle and pushed his hat so that its rim shielded his eyes from the sun.

Suddenly Red started. He shook his head as if to drive reason back quickly. He cursed. He must have dozed. What the hell had wakened him? His senses flooded back. He heard the clatter of horses' hooves and the creak of a vehicle. He pushed himself over and slid up the rock so that he could see further along the trail.

A stagecoach! Red watched with greed and temptation clawing into his mind. It was coming at a steady pace, swaying on the rough road, sending dust billowing behind it. The driver and shotgun rode on top with a few bits of luggage stacked behind them. So there were passengers on board. Red grinned. An opportunity to relieve the monotony and get a few takings into the bargain. They may not amount to much but he'd have some fun relieving the folks of their money and maybe a few trinkets if there were women on board, and it would make a break in the boredom of his vigil.

Red sized up the lie of the immediate countryside and picked out the spot for the hold-up. He slid from the rock and hurried to his horse in the shade of a neighbouring boulder.

He moved carefully towards the trail keeping out of sight of the approaching stage. He gentled his horse through a cleft, a split in the cliff-like rock which towered over trail. He stilled his mount and waited.

The rattle of the coach drew nearer. The horses were moving at a steady trot. Red tuned his ears to the movement. He pulled his bandanna over the lower half of his face. Nearer. Red drew the Colt from the oiled leather of his holster. Nearer. The clatter grew louder. Louder.

Red touched his horse, urging it out of the cleft. He turned it sharply to face the coach. The timing was perfect, and the sudden appearance of a horseman right in his path caused the startled driver to automatically pull on the reins. Jerked by the pull, the horses started to come to a protesting halt. Dust swirled from their grinding hooves. Leather creaked and wood squeaked at the sudden alteration in movement. Wheels skidded, locked by the action of the driver on the brake.

The shotgun, shaken out of his drowsiness, instinctively started to raise his rifle.

Red loosed of a shot over the heads of the men on the coach. 'Drop it!' he yelled.

The shotgun threw down his rifle and raised his hands as the coach came to a swaying halt.

Keeping the two men covered, Red moved alongside the coach. 'Throw down your gunbelts.' As the men started to do as they were told, Red cautioned them, 'Easy like.' Then he added, his call directed to the occupants of the coach, who, startled by the sudden braking and by the shot, were looking out with wide-eyed apprehension, 'You lot, out!'

101

Red inched his horse so that he had everybody covered as they scrambled out of the coach. Four people lined up beside it, two ladies and two men, who immediately raised their hands.

'You two, down beside them,' Red ordered. The driver and the shotgun climbed down and joined the line.

Red swung from his horse and grabbed a bag from the elder of the two ladies. She shrank back in fright and started to whimper. 'Shut up,' snapped Red. 'I ain't going to hurt you.' He turned to the shotgun. 'Here take this and collect their money and jewellery.' The man hesitated. 'Move!' rapped Red with a menacing jerk of his gun. The man went about his task quickly and, though the passengers reluctantly gave up their possessions, they did so without any protest for they feared the menace of the gun.

Red cast a cursory eye over the passengers. Mother and daughter perhaps, the elder woman whimpering with fright, but the younger one, well, he wouldn't mind her for a night, met his gaze with an unscared, defiant look. It came as if she could read his thoughts and dared him to try. He was almost tempted, but he let his eyes slide to the fat man who was obviously scared stiff. It only served to heighten Red's admiration of the girl who showed not one strain of fear. Red cast the fat man a look of contempt and moved to the second male passenger.

Red started. It couldn't be? Red stared hard at the man. It was. He was certain of it. His immediate doubt had only come because the sight was so unexpected. Red stiffened. His mind seathed with hate. His eyes narrowed with malice. Judge Reynolds. The man who had condemned him to that hell-hole of a penitentiary! The man on whom he had sworn to take revenge. What luck. Red couldn't believe it. The man he wanted was here, delivered to him unexpectedly. Red's finger twitched on the trigger of his Colt. It would be so easy. But was that the way he wanted it? Quick, easy? Hell no! He wanted this man to suffer.

'You, where you heading?' demanded Red.

The man hesitated then said, 'North Platte, if it's any concern of yours.'

Red recognized a certain defiance in the attitude of the judge. The man was studying him, but obviously hadn't identified him or else, Red figured, he'd be quaking in his shoes.

Red's eyes narrowed as he thrust his face nearer the judge. 'And there you'll be sending some other poor bastard to the hell-hole of a pen.' He was pleased to see a flicker of alarm cross the judge's face. He turned his head away and snapped at the guard, 'Hurry it up!'

The man scurried to finish his task and then held out the loot to Red. Red took it with his free hand.

'Back on top,' Red ordered indicating the driver and shotgun. The two men scrambled on to the coach. Red turned to the passengers. 'On board.'

The fat man swung round quickly and climbed into the coach without any thought for the ladies. Red caught the glance of the young woman and raised his eyebrows in contempt for the behaviour of the man already aboard. Though she agreed with Red, the girl's face remained impassive. She would share nothing on the criminal's level. She helped the older woman on to the coach and then followed her. The judge moved to the door. Red placed his Colt across the man's chest, stopping the movement. 'Not you,' he hissed.

Reynolds started. He glanced at Red. For one fleeting moment it was a defiant look but then was replaced by anxiety and then by fear. Red smiled. He knew that Judge Reynolds had seen death in the cold steel eyes which stared at him over the edge of the grey bandanna.

'Close the door; you ain't going,' Red ordered.

The judge reluctantly swung the door shut.

'See here, you can't …' The young woman stared down at Red imperiously.

'Can't I?' cut in Red harshly. 'I can and I am. If you know what's good for you you'll keep your tongue tied.' He turned away and called up to the driver. 'Take it away.'

'What about him?' The driver nodded towards the judge.

'He stays with me,' said Red.

'Why? He ain't …' started the driver.

'Not your concern.' Red's lips tightened. His eyes darkened. He was getting fed up with these protests. 'Are you getting on your way or ...' He left the threat unspoken.

The driver, seeing that there was nothing he, or anyone else, could do for the judge, flicked the reins and set his team of horses into motion. The stage creaked and groaned as it gathered momentum. Red, standing slightly behind the judge, watched the coach roll down the trail with the dust beginning to billow behind it.

The judge watched it too but with his heart sinking into icy waters. He had seen a death look in the robber's eyes.

'Move.' Red prodded Reynolds in the back and indicated the cleft down which he had ridden to hold up the stage.

The judge started forward. Red picked up the reins of his horse and followed.

'What's this all about?' asked Reynolds over his shoulder, trying to force his voice on to an even tone.

'You'll find out soon enough,' returned Red.

'Why me? Why not the other man?'

'I've a special interest in you.'

'Me? What?'

'Soon enough. Now shut up and walk.' The judge knew he would get no more, for Red's voice, harsh, menacing, drove the spike of certainty into Reynold's mind.

As they entered the cleft, the robbery planned by Palmer rose in his mind. Had he jeopardized it? No. Nobody could associate the two. Clem and the others need never know he had held up the stage. But now it had become more than a small-time hold-up. Abducting the judge had seen to that. Now there was the greater possibility of a posse searching for the judge. He'd better get this over quick and get clear of the area.

Everything would be all right. Red tried to reassure himself. The stage would reach Glenrock, report the hold-up and abduction but there would be no connection with the big robbery later on.

Besides, what the hell, he was another step along the road to revenge. The next victim would be that damned Cap Millet who had outwitted, and out-gunned him to make his arrest. Well, now, when Millet, wherever he was, heard about the killing of Judge Reynolds, he would realize that a gunman haunted his trail. Red smiled to himself.

The trail steepened between the cleft. The judge stumbled. He lost his hat which rolled back down the slope. He turned to get it.

'You won't need that where you're going,' laughed Red harshly. He motioned the judge onwards.

Reynolds looked at Red. Fear danced in his eyes and his face drained of colour. 'You can't ...'

'Don't tell me what I can and can't do,' snapped Red. 'I've got the power here.' He lifted his Colt menacingly.

The judge stumbled backwards as if somehow that would take the threat away. He fell on his back, staring upwards at the gun which pointed straight at his head.

'No! No!' he cried. His whole body started to shake. 'I'll give you what you want. I'm a man of fair wealth, you can have it all, you ...'

'Shut up.' Red's eyes flared angrily. 'I don't want money you got from enjoying sending men to the gallows or to stew in gaols like that place of lost souls you sent me to. All I want is revenge.' In that moment Red swept the bandanna from his face.

The judge, shocked by recognition, cringed back in horror. Flooding before him was the sight of a face contorted in evil, shouting and yelling threats of revenge as warders dragged Red Collins away to serve his sentence for robbery. Now that face was here before him, still evil but it was the evil of delight in revenge being fulfilled.

'Collins! No, not this way.'

'On your feet, you snivelling bastard!' Red's lips curled with contempt.

The judge twisted over and scrambled to his feet, slipping in his panic. 'They'll catch you. They'll hang you,' spluttered Reynolds grasping at anything which might save his life. There was an ice-cold silence from Red. 'As soon as that coach reaches Glenrock there'll be a posse after you.' The words came thicker and faster as Reynolds saw the seconds of his life moving beyond his reach. 'You won't stand a chance. They'll hunt you down. They'll shoot you like a cur or hang you by your neck.'

'Shut up! Shut up!' yelled Red. He was tired of words pounding at his mind. He kicked out at the judge, catching him behind his left knee.

The man yelled with the pain as he lost his balance and fell heavily. He reached out to his knee, but before he could find small comfort in his touch, Red lashed out with his Colt, drawing the barrel across Reynolds's face. The judge shouted as his brain registered the searing pain. A long gash spurted blood. His fingers automatically came to his cheek and blood oozed between them. He looked up at Red in terror.

'Up,' hissed Red.

Instinctively Reynolds obeyed. He climbed, slithered and stumbled, his whole body shaking with fright, until the slope flattened between the towering walls of rock. He tottered a further hundred yards before Red called a halt.

The rock face on the right had lowered and sloped into a small canyon.

'In there,' Red motioned with his gun.

'No, please, anything, but not ...' cried the judge.

Red's face was filled with hate. His mind held a picture of the harsh, unyielding prison. He would be like that; he would not yield. He pushed the judge towards the canyon.

Reynolds staggered against the rock face, turning, with his back pressed hard against it, in cringing terror.

'Further!' Red pushed him so violently that he stumbled in little running steps until he fell face down. He grovelled in the dust as if that might appease the devil of vengeance who stood over him. 'Turn round, you little runt. Round.' Red kicked him in the ribs. The judge gasped with the pain and rolled on to his back. He stared upwards into the cold barrel of a Colt. Red grinned. 'All the time in that hell-hole of a prison I dreamed of this – of you, of Millet and the prison governor grovelling under my gun. The governor's paid in another way. Now YOU, then Millet.' Red laughed harshly at the abject fear which contorted the judge's face.

He squeezed the trigger. The bullet blasted the man's head open. Blood splattered across the dust. The body jerked. Red fired again and again, the madness of delighted revenge blazing in his eyes. He shoved his Colt back into its holster, turned, walked swiftly to his horse, mounted and headed for camp.

ELEVEN

Wes and Clem unhitched their horses and were about to mount when the distant sound of hard running hooves grabbed their attention.

There was apprehension in their exchanged glance for they sensed alarm in the pounding noise.

Dust billowed beyond the town. They shielded their eyes against the glare of the afternoon sun and recognized the stage.

'Trouble,' frowned Clem. 'Better see what it is.'

They watched the horses hit the main street at a fast run with the driver hauling hard on the reins and yelling to the horses to slow down. Judging his moment right, he applied the brake and brought the swaying coach to a sliding halt outside the stage office.

The noise had brought a few people on to the street. Seeing the stage, they sensed trouble, and were now hurrying to investigate.

'Hold-up!' yelled the shotgun even before the

stage had stopped.

The word spread like a prairie fire, bringing more people on to the street.

Frightened, buffeted passengers, scrambled from the coach. The older woman collapsed in a faint as soon as her feet touched the boardwalk and two ladies stepped forward to help the younger woman administer aid. The fat man, sweating profusely from fright as well as the heat, grabbed the nearest person and poured out a gibbering story. A knot had gathered round the driver. Clem stood on the edge of the group to catch the story while Wes, who waited with the horses, kept an eye open for Cap Millet. Whatever happened, he did not want to be recognized.

A few moments later he saw Cap emerge from the house along the street and hurry in the direction of the throng of people. Wes glanced anxiously at the group. He caught Clem's eye and, with an inclination of his head, indicated him to hurry.

Clem nodded and, a moment later, moved towards Wes.

'Millet's coming,' said Wes, a touch of anxiety in his voice.

'Right, let's ride, but casual, reckon everyone will be too busy to notice us. We'll take the first side street and be out of sight.'

The two men swung into the saddles, sent their horses slowly the few yards to the side street.

Once out of sight of the people of Glenrock and away from possible recognition by Cap Millet, Wes felt easier and able to satiate his curiosity about the stagecoach.

'What was it all about?' he asked.

'Seems a lone gunman held up the stage. Wonder if Red saw it?' said Clem. 'He took money and trinkets from the passengers but then the curious thing was that he kept one of the passengers, a Judge Reynolds, when he sent the others on.'

Wes stopped his horse and stared at Clem in disbelief. Clem halted and turned in the saddle. 'What's wrong?' he queried.

'Judge Reynolds you said?' asked Wes, almost as if he was hoping Clem would deny it.

Clem nodded. 'Yes, Reynolds.'

'Oh, hell! What the devil's Red got up to?' The words hissed from Wes's tightening lips.

Clem frowned. 'What do you mean?'

'Reynolds was the judge at Red's trial. He sent him down and Red swore revenge,' explained Wes.

Clem's eyes widened with comprehension of what might have happened and how it might affect their chance of pulling off Palmer's raid. 'You mean Red held up that stage? But he couldn't know Reynolds was aboard.'

'That's been sheer chance,' said Wes, 'but once he found Reynolds was there …'

'Hell,' gasped Clem. 'There'll soon be a posse out. Let's ride.'

Once clear of the town the two men did not spare their horses.

When they reached the camp Red was crouching close to the fire pouring himself a cup of coffee.

Clem was out of the saddle almost before his mount had stopped. He flew at Red and before Red realized what had happened Clem had grasped his shirt and yanked him to his feet. The tin mug flew from his hand and the coffee pot hit the ground spilling its contents around the fire.

'What the hell have you been up to?' yelled Clem, his face close to Red's.

Startled by the sudden appearance of the two men from Glenrock and by the violence of their boss the other three men jumped to their feet and automatically ranged themselves to the best advantage to support their boss should the trouble erupt further.

Red, startled by Clem's attack, realized Clem and Wes knew he had held up the stage. They must have been in Glenrock when the stage hit town and Wes, on hearing Judge Reynolds mentioned, had drawn the right conclusion. He glanced at Wes who, as one with Clem, faced his brother.

'You've jeopardized Palmer's plan,' snarled Clem. 'How the hell d'you think he's going to take it?'

Over his initial shock, Red's face changed to a mask of defiance. 'We can still do the robbery,

114

nobody's going to associate it with the stage hold-up.'

Clem shoved him away in disgust. 'Hold-up! That was bloody foolish, but murder, that's ...' In his rage Clem was lost for words. 'There'll be a posse out for you and that ain't going to be healthy for us. What the hell are we going to do?'

'Plan as before and ...' started Red.

'Shut up!' The words rasped harshly from Wes. His eyes bore the contempt he felt for his brother. 'You were told to forget revenge but you're too stupid to do that.'

Red swung on his brother. 'You ain't served time in that pen,' he yelled. His face creased with rage. 'If you had you'd have felt like me. Well, I got that bastard of a judge. The governor paid his debt in a different way. Now that leaves Millet.'

'Millet! Tangle with him and you're done,' snapped Wes.

'Like hell. I'll get him,' snarled Red.

'Maybe you'll tangle sooner that you expect,' rapped Wes. 'Millet's in town.'

'What!' Red gasped. His face paled. He seemed to automatically go into a defensive crouch and the men who watched him knew that the name Millet had drained some of the bravado from him, in spite of the swagger he still tried to impart. 'Good, then the bastard's end is near.'

'Forget it.' Clem's voice cut rapier-like into everyone's mind. He glared hard at Red. 'We've come to do a job, and that job we're going to do even though you've made it harder.'

'Maybe he's made it easier,' put in Wes quietly. All eyes turned on him and they saw a thoughtful look in Wes's eyes. 'Sure.' He glanced at Clem. 'That posse's going to come hunting Red, so let him lead them on. That way there'll be less folk in Glenrock tonight.'

For one moment Clem did not fully grasp the significance of Wes's plan but then, as the consequences struck him, he saw its great possibilities.

'You're damned right,' he grinned with enthusiasm. 'Red can lead that posse a dance, keep 'em out of our way, then lose them way up north and double back to meet us at Muddy Gap, top of the pass four days' time.'

'Why not back at the Running W?' asked Dex.

'The way this runt's messing things up I'll have to be certain he ain't followed,' said Clem.

'Hold it.' All eyes turned at the tone of protestation from Red. 'I ain't letting some posse know where I'm heading.'

Clem's eyes fixed him with a penetrating, 'you'll do as you're told' look. 'You will or we'll take you into Glenrock and turn you in. Folks'll believe our story of finding you with the body.'

'You wouldn't!' gasped Red.

'Try us,' hissed Clem.

'I'd blow your robbery,' warned Red.

116

'You wouldn't get the chance,' put in Walt, fingering his knife with meaning. 'Pity you tried to escape before you could blab.'

Red licked his lips. He glanced round the five men. The cold menace in their eyes sent a shiver down his spine. He'd have to play along. But he could lose the posse right away … he slowed his thoughts; he wanted his share of the loot and to keep that posse on the run for a couple of days was his only chance. 'All right,' he agreed.

Plans were made quickly and Red rode away from the camp to lay the trail from the scene of the murder.

When Cap Millet reached the group outside the stage office he quickly grasped the facts about the hold-up. Judge Reynolds abducted. Reynolds! Cap frowned. Why would a small-time thief, for that's what he appeared to be as the stage was carrying no valuables, abduct the judge? Unless he had a vendetta against him. Cap gasped. One name sprang to mind – Red Collins! He recalled Red's vicious threats not only on the judge but on himself. Recently he had heard that Red had escaped from the pen. Could Red have known Reynolds was travelling on that coach or had it been just a coincidence? Probably the latter because if Red had known wouldn't he have just concentrated on the judge and not bothered robbing the passengers? Cap shrugged his

117

shoulders. Whatever, the ways things had happened he was fairly certain this could be the work of Red Collins.

His mind was jerked back to the situation around him when he realized that confusion was reigning.

No one was in charge. Everyone was talking. The word posse was being bandied but no one seemed capable of organizing one.

'Hold it!' Cap yelled at the top of his voice. The authoritative ring took everyone's attention. They turned to see the stranger commanding their attention. 'No lawman here?'

Negative murmurings ran through the crowd.

'I'm an ex-lawman. Want me to take charge?'

'Aye. Sure.' The agreements which flowed were touched with relief.

'All right. We won't gain anything by panicking and rushing off. Let's get the facts first.' Cap turned to the driver and shotgun. 'What can you tell us?'

'Not much,' replied the driver. 'This fella suddenly appeared on the trail through Washout Gulch and got the drop on us before Luke here had a chance to raise his rifle.'

'Can you describe him?'

'Shortish, stocky, couldn't see his face, bandanna, stetson pulled well on. His attitude was mean.'

'Dark brown eyes.' All turned to the young woman from the stage. 'Cold, icy, they could send a shudder through you.'

Cap nodded his thanks. 'Any reason why he should take the judge?' he asked. 'Did he seem to recognize him?'

The driver shook his head. The shotgun screwed up his mouth. Cap glanced at the fat man.

'I can't tell you anything,' he spluttered. 'It was all too horrible.' The man mopped his forehead. 'It's coming to something when you can't travel around in safety. Shouldn't you be out after him now? He's getting further away while you stand here jabbering.'

Cap's lips tightened. His eyes narrowed. 'Do you want to organize a posse?' he rapped.

'No. No. Not me. That's not …'

'Then let me run things my way,' snapped Cap. 'I want to learn what I can about this man. Just how dangerous he is before I lead men into what might be real trouble.' He turned to the girl who had impressed him with her demeanour. 'Anything else?'

'He gave no hint of recognition, but he might easily have hidden his feeling behind his bandanna.'

'Not through his eyes?' asked Cap.

'I couldn't see them when he moved away from me,' she explained. 'He never used the judge's name. After he had got our money and jewellery he ordered us back on the coach. All of us except the judge had got on board. He was about to when the man stopped him.'

119

'I protested,' put in the driver, 'but it was no good. He told me to drive off. Couldn't do anything else, so I hit town as quickly as possible.'

Cap nodded thoughtfully. There was nothing really definite to indicate that it was Red Collins who had held up the coach but that observation of cold, dark brown eyes, coupled with the fact that no petty thief would want to abduct a judge, made Cap feel in his bones that the man they would be looking for was Red Collins.

'Right, will twenty of you ride with me?' His eyes swept the gathering. Murmurs approved his request. 'Get your horses.' As the men hurried away, Cap turned to the coach driver. 'Will you ride with us and show us where the hold-up took place?'

'Sure will.'

Ten minutes later the posse thundered out of Glenrock.

TWELVE

Red rode quickly, cursing Clem for forcing him to do this job and cursing his brother for suggesting it. A decoy, what the hell ...? But even in his suppressed anger he realized that he could provide an ideal opportunity for the robbery at Glenrock to go much easier.

He had been uneasy at the revelation that Cap Millet was in Glenrock. The man had outwitted him once before but now ... As he rode a calmness came to his reasoning. If he played this right he might get even with Millet as well.

Reaching the end of the canyon where he had taken his revenge on Judge Reynolds, Red quickly made a confusion of his previous tracks, without obliterating them, and then, mounting his horse, left a deliberate track back to the scene of the hold-up. From there he left a trail which would be easy to follow once it had been found.

'We're nearly there,' called the stage driver,

'better hold back, there may be tracks.'

Cap signalled the riders to halt and, as their horses milled around, he instructed them to wait while he examined the ground.

He and the driver rode forward slowly until they found the tell-tale marks indicating the place of the hold-up. Cap slid from the saddle and examined the ground more closely. In a few moments he picked up the trail of the two men. He started towards the cleft in the rock wall.

'Four of you follow me. The rest wait,' he shouted to the posse. He tossed his reins to the stage driver.

Four men dismounted and hurried after Cap. As they climbed the slope Cap noticed two sets of hoof marks going down but only one going up. That going up was in keeping with the two sets of footmarks which did not always stick to a set pattern. Those coming down were much more of the pattern of a ridden horse. Cap judged one must have been formed when the robber rode to hold up the coach, the other must be after ... Cap did not dwell on what he expected to find.

The group saw the foot tracks turn into a narrow canyon. The horse had not been taken in. Cap moved cautiously in the lead but only a few footsteps brought him to a halt. A body lay spreadeagled, the head blown open by a shot at close range. Even the toughened Cap shuddered

The others gasped at the mutilated form and some swore a horrible vengeance on the killer.

'So that's what we're up against,' said Cap sharply. 'Let's get him out of here.'

One man peeled off his shirt and covered the head with it. The body was carried back to the waiting men in silence.

'Two of you take the body back to town,' ordered Cap. 'The rest ride with me.'

As two men prepared to leave for Glenrock, Cap cast around to try to pick up the hoof marks which had been made after the killing. He cast wide, away from the actual scene of the robbery. After a few minutes he straightened with a smile of satisfaction. He called to the posse who joined him as he mounted his horse. He steadied the animal as he addressed the men.

'We're dealing with a vicious killer. I think I know his identity. Red Collins. I took him in after a bank robbery. Judge Reynolds sent him to the pen. He swore revenge on both of us. I heard he'd escaped the pen. How he knew the judge was on that coach is a mystery.'

'Maybe it was chance,' someone called.

'Could be,' agreed Cap. 'But, whatever, if we have to split I don't want anyone tackling him on his own; get help. Any questions?' Cap glanced round the posse and when there were none forthcoming he said, 'Let's ride,' and turned his horse along the trail to the north.

Throughout the rest of the daylight hours they followed the trail easily and were encouraged in their efforts when they twice sighted a lone rider who, suddenly aware of their presence, took evasive action.

With the last rays of the sun sinking below the horizon, leaving a sky shot with red and gold, Cap called a halt.

'We'll make camp for the night,' he said as the riders milled around him.

'Shouldn't we go on?' someone called. 'He can't be far ahead.'

'We won't be able to follow his trail in the dark,' pointed out Cap.

'If we camp he'll get further ahead, maybe give us the slip completely,' another voice put in.

'He'll be as tired as we are and so will his horse,' replied Cap. 'He'll hole up for some sleep. Now let us do the same.'

Darkness held the Wyoming countryside in a stilled peace when five riders approached Glenrock at a walking pace.

Half a mile from town Clem called a halt.

'You know where you've got to be?' he said keeping his voice low.

Each man murmured his acknowledgement recalling the plan of the town which Clem had drawn when he instructed them in the way they would carry out the robbery.

'Right, then let's go.' The party split, with only Clem and Wes riding directly into town. They had judged correctly. The town was hushed. The odd light shone from private houses and the only lights in the centre of town shone from the saloon and the hotel. The latter was silent and only an odd voice could be heard drifting from the saloon now and again.

'Figure the posse found Red's trail and are camping out for the night,' commented Wes.

Clem nodded. 'Suits us fine.'

The townsfolk had been shocked by the arrival of two of the posse with the body of Judge Reynolds and an uneasy pall of tragedy cloaked Glenrock.

As they crossed the intersection at the centre of town a figure stepped into the open and almost immediately melted into the shadows again. Clem and Wes knew that Walt covered their rear.

Not wanting to draw attention to themselves they kept to a walking pace. As they passed the livery stable another figure appeared momentarily and they knew that Dex had dealt with any guard that there might have been on the wagon which they could see parked beside the corral fence at the rear of the stable. They slipped from the saddles. Cadiz moved out of the gloom to take charge of them. He soothed them with a gentle voice as Wes took the dynamite from the saddle bags.

Without a word Clem and Wes hurried to the wagon. Wes examined the steel construction quickly.

'A tough job,' he frowned. 'Let's see what it's like underneath.' He crawled under the wagon and reappeared a few moments later with a nod of satisfaction. 'Weakest part's across the axle. Figure we can do it from there.'

'Good,' said Clem. He gave Wes an encouraging pat on the shoulder and turned to keep watch on the immediate surroundings knowing that Dex would be covering the rest of the main street.

Lying on his back, Wes carefully fastened the dynamite at three places alongside the axle. He was having to use more dynamite than he had expected but it was no good unless he blew a manageable hole in the wagon. Having secured the dynamite he ran out the fuse as he scrambled from under the wagon. He climbed to his feet and in a half crouch he moved backwards reeling out the fuse as he went. He took it to the side of the stable, signalled to Clem who moved swiftly to join him.

'Ready,' whispered Wes.

Clem licked his lips and nodded.

Wes scratched a match with his thumbnail. It flared, spluttered and settled to a steady glow. Shielding the flame with his cupped hand, Wes lowered it to the end of the fuse. For a moment nothing happened, then the fuse fizzed and started on a sparkling trail across the ground. Both men watched, mesmerized by the sparks racing towards the wagon.

Wes started. His mind pounded at him 'Get the hell out of here.' He tapped Clem on the arm bringing him back to the threat of the moment. Both men raced round the end of the livery stable and flung themselves flat on the ground close to its wooden wall.

The seconds seemed like an eternity. Then the whole earth vibrated with a booming explosion. The livery stable shook under the blast and Glenrock reverberated with the sudden disturbance.

Clem and Wes jumped to their feet, oblivious to the noise of the frightened horses in the stable. They raced into the open at a dead run for the wagon. Debris was still falling amidst the dust which was settling thickly.

The wagon was over on its side and the force of the explosion had lifted it several feet away.

When he saw the gaping hole in the bottom, Wes felt some sense of satisfaction at a job well done.

'Nice work,' yelled Clem.

Timed to perfection, Cadiz appeared with their horses, as the two men dragged six sacks from the wagon. They slung two over each animal and passed two to Cadiz. Wes and Clem swung into the saddles and sent their horses racing away from Glenrock.

The explosion sent shock waves through the inhabitants of Glenrock. Dazed and bewildered, people raced outside, trying in their bufuddled minds to comprehend what had happened. They were only half aware of the pound of hooves fading into the darkness.

But in a few moments word spread with the quickness of a prairie fire that the wagon which had been driven in earlier in the day by three men had been blown up. All the townspeople had known was that it must carry an important load seeing that it was made of steel and that a guard had been posted.

Two of the men came running to the scene. Though shocked and amazed at the gaping hole and that the six sacks were gone, they instigated an immediate search for their companion. Within five minutes, to their relief, he had been found in one of the stalls in the livery stable, unconscious, but no worse.

'Jake, look after Pete, I'm going to see if I can pick up the trail of these bastards.' The taller of the two men spoke with an authoritative tone marking him out as the man in charge of the wagon.

'Right, Clay,' Jake acknowledged.

'I'll come with you.' The stage driver, who had returned to Glenrock with the judge's body, had pushed his way through the crowd. 'If we can't pick up a trail I reckon we'd better push on and find the posse to inform them what's happened. There's an ex-lawman riding with them.'

Clay agreed and the two men soon had horses

saddled and were riding away from Glenrock still dazed under the events which had so quickly brought upheaval to a town which until now had let the world pass by and kept itself to itself.

THIRTEEN

Cap woke as the pale wash of dawn touched the horizon and slowly painted the sky with a new day.

He soon had the rest of the posse on their feet and in the saddle. He wanted to be close to the killer as soon as possible. He picked up the trail easily and within half an hour came upon the cooling ashes of a camp-fire. Cap cursed. The killer must have started before sun-up.

The posse rode steadily, united in a positive determination, grim with the knowledge of the slaughter.

Twenty minutes later Cap called a halt. Ahead the killer's progress was lost in a mass of hoof marks made by milling horses, or was it the work of one horse whose rider was bent on covering his tracks? Cap was beginning to have his suspicions. He felt that the killer was leaving a trail easy to follow. But why?

'Reckon we've lost it,' someone called.

Cap, his face clouded with annoyance, nodded.

He quickly took in their surroundings. On either side of the trail, bare rock rose gradually. Though smoothed by wind and rain, it was still rough enough to afford a grip for a horse, yet its very nature made it difficult to pick up a trail. The killer could have taken any direction.

Cap was about to split the posse up when the distant pound of hooves signalled riders in a hurry. The posse checked their milling mounts and turned to see who hadn't time to waste.

Two riders came in view. They did not spare their horses even when they saw the group filling the trail, in fact the sighting seemed to spur them on.

'Stage driver!' someone called in surprise.

A puzzled murmur ran through the posse.

'Who's with him?'

No one answered.

The obvious urgency of the approaching riders raised a sense of disquiet. Something was wrong. Each man waited with irritation, wanting an answer before they could get it.

Then the two men were close, reining their horses to a dust-stirring, sliding halt.

'Been a robbery back in Glenrock,' called the stage driver.

A gasp ran through the posse.

'This here's Clay, one of the guards on a wagon which stopped for the night,' the driver went on.

Clay quickly informed the posse of the facts. Bewilderment clouded the riders.

'Killer or robbers, who do we hunt?' someone queried.

'Hold it!' yelled Cap above the questions which had started to fly. His sharp voice of authority brought quiet. 'Clay, you say dynamite must have been used?' Cap's statement was tinged with query seeking confirmation.

'Must have. No other way into that wagon,' said Clay.

'What were you carrying?'

'Cash.'

Cap's lips tightened. 'Damn, damn. I figure we've been taken for suckers.'

The men looked at him in surprise. 'You figure the killing and robbery are linked?' someone asked.

'A year or so back I brought in Red Collins after a bank robbery,' explained Cap. 'He swore vengeance on myself and the judge, and that judge was called Reynolds.'

'So you think the killer you've been trailing is this Red Collins?' said Clay.

'Has the makings,' replied Cap. 'He had a brother, Wes, not really bad like Red but he was good with dynamite.'

'Then you figure he might be involved in the robbery,' Clay added.

'Could be,' said Cap.

'You reckon the killing of the judge was to get the menfolk out of town?' the stage driver asked.

'Don't see how it could have been planned,'

133

puzzled Cap. 'But whatever, it happened and I figure the robbers used it.'

'Smart,' mused Clay. 'So what now? I'm more concerned about that cash.'

'Did you pick up any trails?' queried Cap.

'No. That's why we rode for you, you being an ex-lawman. Apart from that we figured the posse would want to get back to town, a few buildings have been damaged.'

'Right,' agreed Cap. 'We'll all ride back.'

'What about the killer?'

'Let me play a hunch,' said Cap. 'I stopped over in Glenrock on my way to Greeley. The money from that robbery when I caught Collins was never recovered. We figured Wes had it and he got away and dropped out of sight. A week back I heard tell he might be in Greeley, going straight, running a livery stable. I was on my way to check it out. Always rankled with me that the money was never recovered. If this latest use of dynamite is his work then I may get a lead in Greeley. Let me try.'

The men of Glenrock agreed. They wanted to get back to their mundane lives, with no upheavals. Though they wanted a killer brought to justice they had no stomach for a long trail.

Clay agreed with Cap. He would have to report to his authorities as quickly as possible. Besides with no robbers' trail to follow he had nothing to lose in letting Cap follow up a lead, tenuous though it was.

Once back in Glenrock Cap lost no time in

134

gathering his few belongings and setting out along the trail to Greeley.

Three days later, in the chill of the high mountain pass at Muddy Gap, Clem and Wes rode into the camp already set up by Dex and Cadiz. Ten hours later Walt's arrival brought them news of the posse's return to Glenrock.

'Got it from an old prospector back on the trail,' he explained.

Within four hours the sound of an approaching rider alerted them. Cadiz, on lookout, signalled to them that there was no need for alarm. The rider had been recognized and in a few minutes they were greeting Red.

'You ain't been followed?' queried Clem as Red swung from his horse.

'What the hell d'you think I am?' snapped Red, brushing past Clem and reaching for the coffee.

'See anything of Millet?' asked Wes.

'Sure, I saw him,' said Red, over his shoulder, as he crouched beside the fire seeking warmth.

'You didn't do anything damn foolish?' asked Wes, a touch of alarm in his voice.

'I was tempted to take the bastard,' said Red straightening. He eyed his brother meaningfully. 'No, I didn't. But one day I will.'

Wes turned away without comment.

Red glanced at Clem. 'What about the cash? I'll take my pay now.'

A half smile flicked Clem's lips. 'Matt Palmer'll pay you. No one else.'

'Then let's ride, the sooner I get paid the sooner I can go a-hunting clever Mister Millet,' said Red.

'Suits me,' said Clem. 'Let's go.'

Dex kicked the fire embers as the others started to their horses.

'Hold it.' Wes's voice arrested their movements. They turned to him. He looked at Clem. 'I ain't riding with you. I'm heading home.'

'Your pay?' queried Clem.

'You heard me tell Palmer I don't want any,' replied Wes. 'Tell him I kept my bargain. I expect him to keep his.' He glanced meaningfully at Red.

'Palmer will; he always does,' assured Clem.

'Not sure Red merits it really,' said Wes. He started for his horse.

Red's lips tightened. His eyes narrowed at the comment. He started to reach for Wes but Cadiz gripped his arm. 'Leave him,' he hissed. 'Your brother's straight up.'

The six men were soon in the saddles and as five of them headed for the Running W one turned for a lonely ride to Greeley.

The sound of approaching horses brought Matt Palmer on to the veranda. A smile broadened when he saw five riders, with sacks across their saddles.

'Come on in,' he invited, as the riders swung to the ground.

A few minutes later the sacks were dumped on the floor of Palmer's room.

'Where's Wes?' he queried.

'Gone home,' explained Clem. 'Told me to tell you he kept his bargain and expects you to keep yours.'

'Sure,' Matt shrugged his shoulders. 'If that's how he wants it. I figured he wasn't really into this job, but he must have done a good one.' He indicated the sacks.

'Sure did,' said Clem.

'Right, let's see how rich we are,' Matt grinned.

The five men grabbed a sack. Each slit it open without ceremony and tipped the contents on to the floor. Bundles, neatly tied, scattered across the carpet. With an eager excitement, which anticipated good times ahead, they reached for the cash.

They froze. The grins disappeared from their faces. Their minds went numb. Their insides churned.

They stared with a disbelieving incredulity at the bundles. The expected crisp new notes were nothing but blank sheets of paper.

Slowly they raised their eyes to Palmer, who stood staring open-mouthed at the bundles.

He clenched his teeth. 'What the hell?' he hissed. His eyes widened angrily. He looked at his men. 'What the hell's happened?'

'Don't know, boss,' said Clem incredulously.

'We've been fooled,' snarled Palmer. 'We've

blown a decoy.' He stared at the bundles again as if his look might turn them into real money. Slowly he saw the funny side of the situation and started to laugh. 'Well, someone was sure smart.'

'It sure weren't you,' snapped Red. 'Pay me, and let me get to hell out of this here charade.'

'Can't pay you,' chuckled Palmer. 'Your cash is right there on the floor. I ain't got any other.'

'Like hell you have,' snarled Red.

Palmer's face tightened. The smile vanished. He sensed the antagonism in Collins. 'I can give you five hundred dollars and that's final. I banked on tens of thousands on that floor but ...' He shrugged his shoulders.

'You hired me ...' started Red.

'For no fixed price,' cut in Matt harshly. 'I busted you out of gaol, that's worth a lot.'

Red's eyes smouldered angrily. His body tensed like a coiled spring. His hand started to move to his holster but in that split second he felt a knife prick his side.

'Don't try it,' hissed Walt, who, sensing Red's animosity towards Palmer, had moved close to Red without Collins being aware of it.

Red froze.

Palmer nodded his appreciation to Walt, cast a contemptuous glance at Red and moved behind his desk. He opened a drawer and drew out a wad of notes. He tossed them on to the desk. 'Five hundred dollars, take it or leave it.' His words were

138

sharp and Red realized there would be no more cash. He hesitated a moment then reached forward and took the money. So he hadn't got the cash he had expected, but he had his freedom and his brother still had the money from the bank robbery. Some of that was rightfully his. He would see that he got it.

Red swung on his heels and without a word strode from the room.

FOURTEEN

Cap Millet rode at a walking pace along the main street of Greeley. Relaxed in the saddle he allowed his eyes to take in the town. The sheriff's office stood across the rutted dust road from the Silver Dollar saloon. Outside the office a man lolled on a chair in the welcome shade of the awning which topped the boardwalk.

Cap noted the star pinned to the man's chest. Although the sheriff appeared to be asleep, Cap guessed that this was just a pose and, no doubt, he had sized up the stranger riding into town.

Cap made to turn his horse in the lawman's direction but before the movement started he checked it. Better play this one alone, at least for the time being. Any obvious involvement of the law at this time might alert the Collins brothers, if indeed they were in Greeley. Cap decided to make his enquiries from sources other than the lawman.

Two blocks beyond the sheriff's office, Cap saw the livery stable and a block closer, on the opposite

141

side of the street, stood the clapboard fronted Cattleman's Hotel. Ideal. He'd be able to keep the livery stable under surveillance from a front room. He'd recognize Wes Collins, if it was he who ran the livery stable. Cap halted his horse outside the hotel.

'You look as if you're staying, mister. Take your horse to the livery?'

Cap glanced down from his saddle to see a bright-faced youngster whom he judged to be about fourteen, gazing up at him with the expectancy of being rewarded for services rendered.

'Sure, why not,' grinned Cap.

'Thanks, mister.' A broad smile split the youngster's face. He ducked under the hitching-rail and steadied the horse as Cap swung to the ground.

'What's your name?' asked Cap as he started to unfasten his belongings.

'Tom, Tom Webster,' came the answer quickly.

The horse nuzzled Tom's shoulder.

'Have a way with horses,' observed Cap.

'Like 'em,' grinned Tom, patting the animal's neck.

'Hope the livery man likes 'em as much as you,' said Cap.

'Mister Conroe, sure does,' replied Tom with enthusiastic assurance. 'Let's me help him at times; knows I love horses.'

Disappointment stabbed Cap's mind. Conroe, not Collins. Then hope. Maybe Wes had changed his name.

'This here Conroe around?' asked Cap.

'No,' said Tom. 'Been away a few days, ain't back yet.'

A touch of excitement flicked Cap's mind. *Been away, not back yet.* Had he been away on a mission which involved dynamite? Could there be a connection between Conroe and Collins? Could they be one and the same man?

'Who looks after the stable when he's away?' asked Cap casually.

'Mrs Conroe with casual help, and I get to do more.'

Cap nodded. He swung his saddle bags over his shoulder. 'Right, you see my horse is well cared for.'

'I sure will. How long you staying, mister?'

'Don't know,' replied Cap. 'I'll let you know when I'm leaving.' Cap stepped on to the sidewalk. 'Here you are, son.' Cap flicked a dollar into the air.

Tom's eyes brightened at the flash of silver. He caught the coin with the touch of an expert. 'Gee, thanks, mister.' He grinned broadly. 'Your horse will sure be all right.' He turned away and started towards the livery stable, with the horse following willingly.

Cap opened the door to the hotel and a few minutes later was dumping his belongings in a first floor front room. His first action was to move to the window to find if it gave him a good view of the main street and a position from which he could observe the comings and goings at the livery stable.

He turned from the window and glanced round the room. It was like hundreds of other hotel rooms throughout the West, spartan but answering the needs of a traveller, a place to lay one's head, a cupboard for belongings, a chair and a table holding a wash basin and a ewer. The room was clean, the bed neat and tidy, covered with a pretty, patterned patchwork quilt.

Cap poured some water from the ewer and washed away the dust of the trail. He changed his shirt, shrugged himself into a leather vest, toyed with the idea of leaving his gunbelt but thought better of it.

Going downstairs he stopped to enquire from the clerk, 'Where's the best place to eat?'

'Golden Sands. Just along from here, opposite the livery stable. Get no better cooking anywhere than Anne Rushforth's.'

'Thanks,' smiled Cap and left the hotel anticipating the food which would satisfy the hunger of a long ride.

The Golden Sands was quiet when Cap strode in. Only two of the twelve tables were occupied, so Cap was able to choose a window table which gave him a view of the livery stable.

Cap studied the hand-written menu which lay

on the spotless table-cloth. A few moments later he looked up when a gentle voice drew his attention.

'Hi. Nice to see you.'

'And you,' replied Cap returning the welcoming smile. It made him feel important, that he was the one who was the focus of attention at that moment.

'New in town?'

'Yes. Hear tell that Anne Rushforth ... that you?' The young woman nodded. 'Well, I hear you're the best cook in town. Hope so 'cos I'm here on business and it might take a few days.'

Anne, enjoying the flattery, laughed, a gentle pleasurable note, which matched the light blue eyes sparkling under thin arched eyebrows set in an oval face. Her dark hair was drawn back and tied at the back of her neck with the remaining length allowed to splay out below her shoulders.

'What can I get you?' she asked.

'Well it all sounds mighty tempting, but I figure right now I'll settle for crispy bacon, lots of bread, three stack pancakes and just keep the coffee coming.'

'Fine. Be with you shortly.' Anne smiled and moved away.

A few moments later Anne was back with a cup and saucer, milk, sugar and a pot of steaming coffee.

'A thriving town,' commented Cap having noted the activity on the main street.

'Sure. We do all right. We're a tolerant lot,'

replied Anne. 'Cater for all tastes. Have a firm sheriff who soon cracks down on any trouble, but generally speaking even the cowpokes who ride in here for a bit of entertainment aren't looking to be a bother.'

'Pretty big livery stable,' observed Cap inclining his head towards the large building across the street.

'Yes. Wes and Kate Conroe have built up a good business since they came here. Nice couple,' said Anne.

'Where did they come from?' asked Cap casually.

'Pine Bluffs, about two years ago. Wes got work with Jake Bell at the livery and when Jake died he left the whole shoot to him.' Anne glanced towards the kitchen door. 'Your food should be ready.' She smiled and turned away.

Cap's mind raced. Anne had called Conroe Wes! If Collins had changed his surname he could still have kept his Christian name. And the Conroes had moved into Greeley not too long after the bank robbery.

As he poured the coffee, Cap wondered if things were falling into place. Well, he would know when Wes Conroe returned. Then maybe his patience would be rewarded.

Three days later, Cap was sitting at a window table in the Golden Sands, sipping his final cup of coffee after enjoying one of Anne's specials, when the sight of a lone rider, easing the stride of his horse to allow two ladies to cross the street, sent his pulse beating faster. He saw the man touch his hat and pass a word with them. Then he rode on. Wes Collins! He was right! His hunch had paid off. Now, if he made his moves cautiously, he'd have Collins behind bars and maybe the money recovered, for Collins hadn't used it to buy the livery stable.

He watched Collins ride past the Golden Sands and saw him turn towards the livery stable.

Maybe this was the time to take him. Cap had seen Kate Conroe go to the livery stable while he was having his meal. In greeting his wife Wes would not be alert for the unexpected. He rose to his feet and took in the scene from the window. Wes Collins was turning in to the livery stable.

Cap hurried from the Golden Sands.

FIFTEEN

Cap walked briskly along the sidewalk until he was opposite the livery stable. He was about to step down into the dust of the rough street when his attention was drawn to a horse coming at a canter. He froze. Though the rider held his head down and his sombrero was tipped forward, he had a familiar look. Red Collins!

Cap stepped back into the shadow of the awning. So the brothers had come back together. But was that so? Their approaches along the main street were so different. Wes came as if he was just returning from a few days away, an easy ride, coming back to the familiar. But Red came as if he was in a hurry, as if he did not want to be recognized, as if this might just be a quick call and away again.

Cap was puzzled. As Red neared, Cap turned away so that his face could not be seen. Out of the corner of his eye he saw Red wheel his horse into the livery stable.

Cap lost no time. He hurried across the street and, hearing voices coming clearly to him, lounged casually against the wall beside the open door so as not to attract the curiosity of anyone on the main street.

'What the hell are you doing back here?' The tone was far from friendly.

'Money, brother Wes, money.' The voice was demanding.

'I thought you'd get enough from Palmer,' said Wes.

Red gave a harsh laugh. 'You pulled out at the right time.'

'I wanted nothing more to do with it. I'd kept my part of the bargain. I didn't want his money,' Wes said.

'You'd have got none. There wasn't any.'

'What!' Wes was astounded. 'All that planning for nothing?'

'Right,' said Red, his tone bitter. 'There was nothing in those sacks but bundles of paper.'

'Bundles of paper!' Wes gasped incredulously. Then, as the amusing side struck him, he started to laugh. 'So Palmer was fooled by a decoy? He went to all the trouble of busting you out of gaol in order to find me to blow up a wagon of useless paper.'

'It ain't funny, Wes,' snapped Red irritably. 'I'm broke. I need cash, so I've come for my share of the bank loot.'

'I told you before, that cash is going back to the

authorities,' replied Wes.

'You've had your share, I want mine,' snarled Red.

'Like I told you, I ain't touched one cent of it.'

'Like hell,' spat Red with a mocking laugh of disbelief. 'What about this stable, you didn't buy this with nuts?'

'Jake Bell, who gave me work here, left it to me in his will,' explained Wes.

'You don't fool me,' rapped Red. 'Now I want my share.'

'I told you, it's going back to the authorities, then maybe they'll forget my part in the bank robbery.' Though the voice was quiet there was a note of sheer determination in it.

Red recognized it. 'Like hell it is. If you don't want it, more fool you, I'll take the lot.'

'You ain't getting it,' hissed Wes. 'If I gave you even your share I could be branded as aiding and abetting a murderer.' Wes's voice went cold. 'Once I knew you'd killed Judge Reynolds, you were finished as my brother.'

'Reynolds got what he deserved,' snapped Red, 'putting me in that hell-hole, and Millet's going to get his.'

'You'd be wiser not tangling with him,' advised Wes.

'I was tempted back on the trail but ...'

'You daren't risk messing up Palmer's plans again,' Wes finished Red's sentence for him.

'Millet can't be far away. I'll pick up his trail and then he'd better watch out. Now, move, the money.'

'You ain't getting it.' There was the ice-edge of certainty in Wes's voice.

'I bloody well am.' Red's Colt sprang to his touch and Wes found himself staring into its cold barrel.

'Wes!' The cry came from Kate who had been left speechless by the revelations of the exchange between the brothers.

'It's all right, love.' Wes tried to sound calm for Kate's sake, though he felt far from it knowing how his brother could react.

'You wouldn't like a shattered kneecap, would you?' barked Red.

'Wes, give him the money,' cried Kate in desperation. She wanted Red gone, far away, to leave them in the peace they had in Greeley until he had appeared like a ghost from the unsavoury past.

'No, Kate,' said Wes quietly.

'A kneecap.' Red's eyes narrowed. 'Money, or else.'

'No!' screamed Kate. She flung herself in front of her husband. 'You'll have to kill me first.' She faced Red defiantly.

'Kate!' Wes grasped her by the shoulders but she resisted his attempt to thrust her out of the way.

'I might just do that.' The ice in Red's voice sent a chill through the stable. 'Unless you know where the money is.'

'I don't,' cried Kate. 'Wes would never tell me.

Said it was better that I didn't know.'

'Then there's only one way.' Red met his brother's wild gaze. 'She's in the way.'

'Hold it!' The voice which rang sharp and clear from the stable door froze the scene.

Red's eyes narrowed. He was tense, alert, sensing danger.

Wes and Kate, though still taut at the nearness of execution, felt relief at the intervention. In it there was a hope for them. But who? Why? They turned to see a shadowy figure step further into the stable.

'Millet!' Red's gasp of surprise came as a hiss of hate.

Wes, recognizing the danger, swung Kate out of the way and dived after her. As they hit the straw in a neighbouring stall the stable was filled with the explosive sound of two gunshots.

Even as he rolled over on to his back and pushed himself to his feet, Wes knew the outcome.

Red lay sprawled in death, thrown to one side by the impact of the bullet. Cap stood, staring regretfully at the body. His right hand, which still held his Colt, grasped his left arm. Blood oozed from between his fingers.

Wes glanced up and met Cap's gaze.

'I'm sorry,' said Cap.

'It was inevitable,' replied Wes.

The clamour on the main street grew louder as Greeley folk rushed to the livery stable to find the reason behind the shooting, something Greeley had not witnessed for a long time.

'I guess you'll take me in, now you've caught up with me,' said Wes, his voice low as he saw his life shattered.

'Oh! No!' the cry came from Kate who had joined her husband. She gripped his arm as if that would prevent an arrest.

Cap eyed the couple. 'I heard all that passed between Red and you. You were going to turn the money in?'

'Sure,' replied Wes. 'Hadn't done it before in case the authorities held me.'

'As far as the folks of Greeley are concerned I caught up with the killer of Judge Reynolds today. You give me the money and I'll turn it into the authorities with some story. No one need ever know that Wes Conroe is really Wes Collins.'